SPECIAL MESSA...

THE ULVERSCR...
(registered UK ch...

was established in 1972 to ...ovide funds for research, diagnosis and treatment of eye diseases. Examples of major projects funded by the Ulverscroft Foundation are:

- The Children's Eye Unit at Moorfields Eye Hospital, London
- The Ulverscroft Children's Eye Unit at Great Ormond Street Hospital for Sick Children
- Funding research into eye diseases and treatment at the Department of Ophthalmology, University of Leicester
- The Ulverscroft Vision Research Group, Institute of Child Health
- Twin operating theatres at the Western Ophthalmic Hospital, London
- The Chair of Ophthalmology at the Royal Australian College of Ophthalmologists

You can help further the work of the Foundation by making a donation or leaving a legacy. Every contribution is gratefully received. If you would like to help support the Foundation or require further information, please contact:

THE ULVERSCROFT FOUNDATION
The Green, Bradgate Road, Anstey
Leicester LE7 7FU, England
Tel: (0116) 236 4325

website: www.foundation.ulverscroft.com

Daniela Krien was born in East Germany in 1975. She studied cultural sciences, communications and media and has worked as an editor and scriptwriter for Amadelio Film. *Someday We'll Tell Each Other Everything*, her first novel, has been translated into fifteen languages.

SOMEDAY WE'LL TELL EACH OTHER EVERYTHING

It is the summer of 1990. The Berlin Wall has collapsed, and Germany is preparing for reunification. Away from this upheaval, young Maria moves in with her boyfriend on his family's farm in the sleepy country-side of the East. A chance encounter with an enigmatic older man ignites an improbable affair. Henner is damaged and unpredict-able, yet Maria is uncontrollably drawn to him. As the summer progresses, keeping their passion a secret becomes ever more difficult. A bold and powerful love story ensues, where violence and desire are in-extricably entwined, painting a portrait of a community in flux.

DANIELA KRIEN

SOMEDAY WE'LL TELL EACH OTHER EVERYTHING

Translated from the German by
Jamie Bulloch

Complete and Unabridged

ULVERSCROFT
Leicester

First published in Great Britain in 2013 by
MacLehose Press
an imprint of
Quercus
London

First Large Print Edition
published 2015
by arrangement with
Quercus
London

A catalogue record for this book is available
from the British Library.

ISBN 978-1-4448-2292-2

Published by
F. A. Thorpe (Publishing)
Anstey, Leicestershire

Set by Words & Graphics Ltd.
Anstey, Leicestershire
Printed and bound in Great Britain by
T. J. International Ltd., Padstow, Cornwall

FOR CHRISTIAN, CLARA
AND ROSA

'And love was the origin of the world and the world's ruler: but all its paths are covered with flowers and blood, flowers and blood'

Knut Hamsun, *Victoria*

1

It is summer, a wonderfully hot summer. At the farm the buildings are ranged around three sides of a yard. In the middle is the long, detached house, which has two floors and a large attic; the barn, on the left-hand side, has large wooden doors at the front and back. A few metres behind it is a wide, low wooden building — the sawmill. Meadows and pastureland stretch down to the river; a short way upstream, just before a weir, is a dilapidated shed. On the far side of the river a densely wooded hillside rises steeply. In the farm building on the right are the cattle and chickens. Behind it, in a raised wooden hut littered with sawdust and hay, live the geese. An extension which houses the vehicles adds a further ten metres to the thirty-metre-long cowshed. The extension also has large wooden doors at both front and back. From its back door, towards the left, you can see the sheep shed bordering the kitchen garden; straight ahead lie fenced meadows, the railway embankment and, some distance beyond the tracks, but clearly visible, Henner's farm.

The Brendels' farm and Henner's farm are

the largest in the village. They say that nothing inside Henner's house has changed since the war: not the furniture, stoves and floors, nor the tiny windows that leak. It must be cold in winter. Everything's more modern at the Brendels'; they've even got central heating. Entering the house on the ground floor you come into a small hallway. To the left and right, doors lead into the kitchen and living quarters; straight ahead is a flight of stairs, and behind the staircase is the door to the kitchen garden and the entrance to the cellar.

Siegfried, Marianne and Lukas sleep in the downstairs bedrooms, Frieda and Alfred have the rooms upstairs, while the attic belongs to us, Johannes and me. The kitchen, the biggest room in the house, still has an old stove you can cook on. But for years now Frieda, the grandmother, has been using the electric cooker. The chairs are older than Frieda, as are the large dining table in the middle of the room and the enormous dresser. Only the wall cupboard and one of the worktops are post-war. Everything is clean and tidy, but it's always gloomy. Now that it's summer, the windows are open most of the time. The windows are old with handles that turn; white paint is flaking off the frame. The low ceiling is oppressive, but also protective.

Siegfried, the father, is sitting at the table. The chestnut tree in the yard gives a dense shade, allowing only tiny scraps of evening light through the windows. Nobody is speaking; the faces of the family are lit so dimly I can hardly recognise them.

One by one the others sit down too. Marianne, the mother; Frieda, the grandmother; old Alfred, who in another era would have been called a retainer; and the sons, Johannes and Lukas.

Siegfried cuts a thick slice from the brown loaf and spreads it with butter. He takes a few slices of red pepper which his wife has cut. He eats slowly and doesn't speak. Then he smiles and says, 'It's great we can buy peppers now, they're very good for you. Did you know that?' He looks up without raising his head.

His sons do not answer. Marianne, his wife, nods and says, 'We'll have many more soon.' Siegfried offers the plate with the peppers to Frieda. 'Try some,' he says with a smile of encouragement.

I look around, trying to understand the rules that govern life here; I haven't lived in the house for long. One Sunday morning in May Johannes said to me, 'I'm not going to take you back home today. My parents want to meet you.' I stayed the night and haven't left since. It's now June.

We go on eating in silence. I listen to the noises the others make as they chew. Alfred is the noisiest. Without looking at Siegfried he mutters, 'Liese's going to calf tonight. She's showing all the signs.' Siegfried nods and peers at the cowshed through the window.

Johannes stands up awkwardly, his head bowed. 'I'm going to meet some friends — in town.'

'On your motorbike?' Marianne asks, getting up too.

'Sit back down!' Now the father's voice has that quiet but menacing tone I like, though it scares me slightly. The others aren't scared.

'Can't I come with you, Johannes?' I ask, fixing my eyes on his bowed head. But he doesn't look at me. Doesn't answer either. He stands there for a moment and then leaves the room. In silence.

★ ★ ★

A road runs past both farms with two narrow tracks leading to the houses. On the other side of the road a lane leads down to the village, about three hundred metres away from the farms. Both sides of the lane are lined with lime trees. Now, in June, they are giving off a heady scent. Near the bridge crossing the river is the tavern which takes its name from these limes.

Further on, the houses and smaller farms, the post office, co-op and church are dotted around the village pond. Narrow lanes snake their way between the buildings, leading to more houses and farms. But one of them goes dead straight from the centre of the village to two low concrete structures that look as if they'd fallen into the field accidentally — the headquarters of the collective farm. The huge collective pig shed towers proudly behind.

It's an unusual village. It survived the war and the G.D.R., as Frieda likes to say. Apart from the odd house and the collective farm H.Q. there's little that's modern. There aren't many places like it any more, and at weekends people come out here from town for a walk.

★ ★ ★

The chickens are running around outside in the yard. Marianne forgot to lock them in. Frieda looks out of one of the upstairs windows and shouts, 'Marianne, the fox is going to have those chickens! After twenty years you still haven't got it: when it's dark the chickens have to be put in their coop.'

5

The old chestnut tree casts a shadow over the entire house. But Siegfried told us it's going to be cut down soon. He wants to plant a new tree; the old one has grown too big.

Marianne goes as far as the barn, just in time to see her son race away on his shiny black M.Z. I've wrapped a scarf around my shoulders; I found it in Marianne's wardrobe. I watch her from the front door. 'Suits you,' she says when she comes back, adding, 'He'll be fine.'

I'm not worried. She's the one who can't relax until he's back home. There have been several fatal accidents on the road recently. Including one of Johannes' friends. I stand there calmly, puffing cigarette smoke into the fresh country air, then I help put the chickens away.

★　★　★

It is almost midnight when I hear the rattle of his motorbike, and then, finally, the engine dying out. The attic rooms store the heat of the day; I've swapped my summer dress for a white nightdress I found in one of the many chests in the attic. It must have been Frieda's once.

If I look out of the back window, I can see the rushing river and rolling countryside stretch out before me; I can see the woods and the cows in the meadows. Out front I look onto the farmyard and the chestnut tree, which is full of birds. From the window in the gable I can see the pasture, sheep shed, railway tracks, and beyond these Henner's farm. I never realised how beautiful this landscape was until I moved in here. For the moment I can think of no better place to live.

But now it is night-time and all I can see is Johannes pushing his bike into the shed. When he comes back out, he lights a cigarette and looks up. He can't see me. I've turned out the light so I don't have to look at the endless procession of spiders descending from the ceiling on transparent threads. They give me the creeps, and I know he finds this childish fear of mine ridiculous.

He's been in town, with his artist friends.

When he comes into the room I pretend to be asleep. He chucks his clothes on the floor and goes to brush his teeth — not for long enough, as usual. It's late and we've got to set off early tomorrow. I'm going to lie again and say I don't have to be in until third period; I'll just stay in bed until he comes back. Johannes is in his final year; we go to the same school. He's in the twelfth year and I'm in the tenth. When I was still living with my mum and grandparents, my journey to school began

7

with a forty-five minute march down the hill to our local town, followed by a bus ride to the county town. Altogether it took me about an hour and a quarter. And the journey home was even slower as I had to go back up the hill.

Now Johannes takes me to school on his bike, but I haven't been going in that often recently. I've lost count of the number of lessons I've missed. I know I'm going to fail at the end of the year. My mornings are spent reading and smoking; in the afternoons we go for rides in the country, sometimes to the artists' café in town, where even though it's still early we drink wine and vodka, and people talk and talk and talk. Johannes likes it, but I don't really know what to make of it.

Then we climb the stairs to our spiders' nest and make love. Johannes turns out the light, he's gentle and tender in bed; he never hurts me. He's the first man I've had. I think I love him.

2

At ten o'clock the following morning — Johannes left for school long ago — the floor vibrates beneath my bare feet. I'm standing at the washbasin in front of the mirror, proudly brushing my long hair. But I can't ignore the knocking coming from the room below. It's Frieda. She's in Alfred's room, a broom in her work-worn hands, thumping the end of it against the ceiling. I have no choice but to go downstairs. If I don't she'll start banging a cooking spoon against the heater. She knows I'm skiving off school. She doesn't approve, but seeing that I am here I might as well help her with the cooking. Frieda is a practical woman.

My book is on the sill of the gable window; I had wanted to go and read in the garden. I'm annoyed at Frieda now, but what's the point? The fate of Dmitry Karamazov will have to wait until the potatoes have been peeled and the onions chopped.

Poor Dmitry, will Grushenka give you the answer you desire?

★　★　★

I knock three times against the heater with the wooden handle of my hairbrush, to let her know I've understood. I mustn't stamp my feet or paint will flake onto the floor, and Alfred will have to sweep it up. Before I go I open the windows, water the lavender in the window boxes and smoke my first cigarette of the day. I get a fantastic rush, which makes me lose my balance; I lean on the windowsill for support and look out at the yard. Marianne is beside the cowshed, admiring the new calf. Liese did it! From three to five o'clock this morning she laboured, eventually giving birth to a healthy calf, though not without some help. Siegfried went in around four o'clock, observed her for a good while, then pulled the long rubber glove over his powerful arm, tied a cord around the calf's front legs and hauled it out. Now it's standing unsteadily beneath its mother, suckling its first milk. It's a sunny day. Later on maybe we'll lie by the river and I'll run my fingers through Johannes' blond hair. This seems to be the only thing he's inherited from his father, the thick blond hair. When the heat gets too much we go to the old shed by the weir and make love. That's what Marianne calls it when Johannes and I are having a bath together and she's behind the bathroom door, which you can't lock: 'Are you making love in

10

there, or why is it taking so long? Siegfried will be up in a minute, and he shouldn't be seeing you naked, Maria.' I can't help giggling, and Johannes puts his head under the water.

★　★　★

Lunch is stew, with meat slaughtered on the farm, of course. I'm actually a vegetarian. I haven't touched meat since that Easter Sunday when Grandma Traudel roasted my favourite bunny, Matze. It was only after lunch that Grandpa Lorenz told me, and I promptly brought poor Matze straight back up again. I was twelve at the time, and that's almost five years ago.

Siegfried doesn't like vegetarians, even though I'm the first he's met. On Sundays he puts the best piece of meat on my plate without saying a word and I put it back, just as silently. I've secretly tried it a few times, and it tastes really good.

Nobody says much — they never do. Siegfried is a man of few words, like most people in the village. But when he does speak we shut up and listen, even if he's talking nonsense. But that's seldom.

He looks tired. He's already been on his feet for eight hours, and he will be for eight more. Tree trunks have to be made into planks in the sawmill, the sheep must be taken to another meadow, a broken fence needs repairing and the cowshed needs mucking out. Milking happens twice a day: at five in the morning and five in the afternoon. The milk lorry comes every other day and empties the chilled tank.

Marianne has work to do in the shop. In spring Siegfried converted the storeroom next to the kitchen into a small farm shop. It's absolutely tiny, not even nine square metres. A narrow white door, open during the summer, leads into a windowless room whose walls are lined with simple shelves made of beeswaxed timber from the farm's own sawmill. Here you can buy the farm produce: eggs, milk, bread baked by Frieda, fresh lamb, beef, chicken and charcuterie, fruit and vegetables, stockings made from the farm's wool. Later in the year, in the run up to Christmas, there are geese for sale too. Lambs and cattle are slaughtered off the farm, chickens and geese in the cellar.

On entering the shop you hear the low tones of a wind chime, the first thing Marianne bought in the West, a few months after the Wall came down. All those events went practically unnoticed here on the farm. They stared at the television pictures from

Berlin as if they were from another country. Frieda said, 'I don't believe it,' Marianne cried, and Siegfried nodded. He kept moving his large head up and down, then went out to feed the animals. This is how Johannes tells it; back then he could hardly contain his excitement and was desperate to get to Berlin. But Siegfried didn't let him go.

★ ★ ★

We're sitting at the table, Siegfried and Frieda at either end, Alfred and Marianne with their backs to the window, and me opposite them. The sons are still at school. Despite feeling exhausted Siegfried is in a good mood. He looks suggestively at his wife. She just smiles back. It is summer 1990. Hay-turning time.

★ ★ ★

In the afternoon we're all in one of the largest meadows by the river with our hay rakes. Siegfried, Frieda, Marianne, Lukas, Johannes, me and Alfred.

Alfred has spent his whole life here. He only left the farm once, and that was for just a few weeks.

Alfred's mother, Maria, was a kitchen maid.

In 1933 she married Alwin, a farmhand. Five months later Alfred was born. Frieda was three at the time; there are pictures of her, a small, round girl with fat plaits and a marked passion for little Alfred. She was the younger of the two Schenke sisters. Anneliese was already at school, whereas Frieda spent from morning till evening dragging little Alfred around the farmyard, putting him to bed amongst the wild flowers, or pushing him around the vegetable garden in a small wheelbarrow. Frieda's brothers had both died of influenza, one aged three, the other five. The boys' bodies were dressed in their Sunday best, and their pictures were taken for the first and last time by a professional photographer from the small town of G. The photographs were framed and hung above the linen chest in the parlour.

★　★　★

Sweat is running down my face. Reluctantly I run back to the house to fetch a headscarf, like the other women are wearing. My eyes are burning from the hay dust flying around; my legs, covered in mosquito bites and scratched by the hay, are horribly itchy. The raking is such hard work it's almost unbearable. In spite of her sixty years, Frieda toils away tirelessly and without complaint.

Even Marianne grafts in silence. Johannes cautions me with a glance; it can't be any later than four, we've got hours to go yet. I catch sight of Alfred taking a hip flask from his pocket and enjoying a furtive glug. I'm thirsty too, and Frieda must be a mind reader. She stops work, leans on her rake and calls out to me, 'Why doesn't she go to the kitchen and fetch us some bottles of water and sandwiches. We'll have a break.'

'Yes, of course!' I reply, and speed across the meadow to the house.

★   ★   ★

When I come back the saws in the mill are running. We women are now alone in the meadow. Well, not entirely alone; Alfred's still here, but he doesn't count. The only thing Alfred does of his own accord is drink, and people here accept it as silently as they do almost everything else. Otherwise he's wholly subservient to Frieda, and has been ever since she used to drag him, the maid's infant, across the farmyard. It's far too late now for a bid for freedom. Without a wife or children of his own Alfred has become an appendage to the family, who have treated him as if he were their own son. After the death of the Schenke brothers he was the only boy around, and his

15

real parents hoped that by entrusting their son to the care of Ingeborg and Wieland Schenke, he might enjoy a better future. Frieda loved little Alfred above anything, and they probably thought — who knows? — perhaps she'd still love him later on, when she was of an age to get married and take over the farm. In fact rumours still persist that Volker, Frieda's eldest, is Alfred's son. He's a drinker too, at any rate. But in the end she married Heinrich Brendel, the strapping, capable son of the village teacher. He too played in the farmyard as a boy, and young Frieda mothered him with an equally ruthless passion, which transformed itself into selfless love and devotion the moment Frieda turned seventeen. In time the Schenkes' farm became the Brendels' farm.

Frieda's first son, Volker, was born shortly after her marriage to Heinrich in 1948. A few weeks before the birth Alfred suddenly disappeared — was this a clue as to the true identity of the father? Frieda denied it vehemently, and so a mantle of silence was laid over this unwelcome speculation. Sometime later Alfred turned up again, ragged and scrawny — like a maltreated dog. His mother collapsed at the stove at the sight of him.

★　★　★

All of a sudden Marianne flops down onto a pile of hay. Her red headscarf has slipped back and you can see her thick hair. She looks young lying there, her lips wet with water; her skirt has ridden up to reveal a strong pair of legs. She's thirty-nine, her two sons eighteen and twelve. 'Mum,' Johannes says, 'your skirt . . . ' She laughs and takes another big swig from the bottle. Then she stands up again and peers over to the sawmill. 'I'll be right back,' she says as she leaves. 'It won't take long.' Johannes sits beside me and puts his head in my lap. I wash the dust from his face with a handful of water and lay my cool hands on his eyes. To my left I can sense Lukas watching us. Leaning on her rake, Frieda is staring at the river; she stands with her legs apart, as if her feet were rooted in the earth. We follow her gaze, but can't make out anything in particular — just the water flowing by, as it does every day. Over in the mill the machines have gone quiet.

★ ★ ★

It's already gone ten by the time we sit at the dining table. Thin slices of cold roast meat have been arranged on a large china platter. Beside this is a basket of dark bread, a ceramic pot of butter, a bottle of wine and a lemon cake. I eat as if I'd been fasting for days; I even help myself to a piece of meat. This earns me a nod of approval from Siegfried. He says we need more help for the harvest; it's about time Volker showed his face again. But Volker's not here, Frieda says in an irritated tone. Siegfried's brothers are Frieda's Achilles' heel. Volker, the eldest, got a job working in the pig sheds at the agricultural collective when he was sixteen. That's where he and a handful of others got into drinking. Now he lives in a small flat in the county town and he's not working any more, even though he's only just turned forty-two. He doesn't have a wife or children. His story sounds so similar to Alfred's that there is always an embarrassed silence when discussion turns to Volker. Then Alfred smiles at Frieda, and she punishes him by ignoring him. Hartmut, the middle son, was just eighteen in 1967 when he submitted an application to leave the country, the contents of which led to his immediate arrest. Two and a half years later the state sold him to the West, without Frieda and Heinrich knowing anything of it. They heard nothing from him again until he found work and somewhere to live in Rosenheim, Bavaria. Frieda still reproaches him for not confiding in her his plans to leave the country. On the other hand her husband,

Heinrich, who died of cancer a few years ago, was proud of his son to the last, even though he never saw him again.

After a glass of wine I feel more tired than I have ever done in my life. It's my first summer on the Brendels' farm, my first summer without my mother, my first summer with a father, even though he's not my own.

After dinner we haul ourselves upstairs and go to bed without washing, without even brushing our teeth. Before I am overwhelmed by an inconceivably deep sleep I decide to skip school tomorrow. The holidays start next week and there's not much point — this year is a write-off anyway.

3

I wake up and find myself alone. Johannes has gone to school.

Today I need to find out whether Alexey Karamazov will get to the monastery before the Elder Zossima dies. And why did Zossima prostrate himself before Dmitry? The sun is high in the sky; it must be almost noon. Downstairs in the kitchen a place has been laid for me, there are rolls in a wooden bowl, chilled butter and home-made jam — the first batch of the summer. In the hallway Siegfried greets me with an unusually friendly smile, and I can hear Marianne cackling away in the shop. Selma the cat rubs up against my legs, which are covered in scratches from yesterday's hay-turning. I've hardly ever felt so happy. My cheeks are tanned; my arms and neck are actually dark brown, even though summer has only just begun.

The door through to the shop is open. Marianne is laughing. She's joking with Henner. I expect he's flattering her. Marianne is still a beautiful woman, powerfully built with a long, thick, dark plait and rosy cheeks. She has a soft spot for Henner. He's buying bread, but maybe he's just come for a chat, he's that lonely. Frieda says that Henner's a wild one. Ever since his wife left him, many years ago now, he's apparently been pretty feral. He inherited the farm from his father and managed to run it down in just a few years. At least that's what they say in the village. The only thing he's got a knack for is horses, in fact you might call it a passion. They're meant to be some of the finest Trakehners around.

Siegfried says it was the G.D.R. that broke him. Someone with his strength should be cultivating his own land, not working in the collective. A man like Henner should be his own master.

Sometimes when he's chasing women or going on a bender he even forgets to feed his dogs. They roam free and kill sheep. Siegfried has also lost lambs to those mastiffs, so he won't be pleased to see his wife joking with that brute. But still, Henner's a handsome man, and well read, they say. He's got shelves of books in his house, and that's not something you see very often round here. The villagers say he takes after his mother, who was a girl from town and quite eccentric too.

'Is Maria still with you?' I hear him say. 'You've got yourselves a pretty one there.'

He roars with laughter and Marianne says, 'She's a lovely girl alright, but she's not cut out for the farm.'

'I can imagine,' he says. 'She won't stay. She'll go off to college and study something, you mark my words.'

'I know, but what can we do? Johannes is besotted by the girl. She skips school and spends all day reading.'

'Is that right?' he says. 'Send her to work in the cowshed, she'll soon forget all about reading, ha ha . . . '

'You're one to talk . . . ' There's a hint of a sneer in Marianne's voice. 'You've always got your head in some book. But let's not go on about it, Henner, things will work themselves out. She hasn't had it easy at home.'

My feeling of happiness is deflated. I leave my roll and go into the shop. They stand there and look at me. 'I heard it all,' I say, jutting out my chin.

'Well,' Henner says, 'she's got a cheek, that girl, but she's damn pretty. Johannes has good taste.'

He looks me up and down shamelessly, Marianne frowns, and I grant him a smile before going out into the yard.

★   ★   ★

Young Karamazov has made it. Zossima is still alive, but when he dies something incredible happens.

22

I need to make myself useful. No-one here takes me seriously, and maybe they're right not to. I go into the garden and fetch some onions, kohlrabi and carrots. Frieda is busy in the kitchen. She's making such a racket with the pots and pans you can hear it in the vegetable garden behind the house. Some post came earlier. From her son Hartmut in Rosenheim. Later I'll see the letter lying there opened. I'll take it out of the envelope and read:

Dear Mother,
I never thought I'd be able to visit you again. But how things have changed. Germany is becoming one country again. Dad would have been very happy. I don't really know what to say — so much time has passed, and I'm not good at writing letters. I'd pre-fer to talk to you. If it's alright with you I'd like to come back home for a visit in the third week of July. I'm going to bring the family, my wife Gisela and the children, Robert and Anna. You have no idea how excited I am. Please forgive me for not having told you anything back then. I would have put you all in danger. I wrote to you from prison, but they didn't send my letters. I wrote again later too, but never got a reply.

I'm really sorry about everything. It's taken all my courage to write this letter, even though I haven't heard anything from you in twenty years.
Your son,
Hartmut

P.S. If I don't hear from you I'll assume that the third week of July is fine. We'll arrive on Monday, but certainly not before midday. It's quite a long drive.

Frieda is sitting at the dining table when I come in. I drop the vegetables on the table and say, 'I'm cooking today.' I notice that she's been crying. She's holding a crumpled handkerchief in her wrinkled hands. Her narrow lips arch inwards — she must have forgotten to put her dentures in. Her grey hair, tied up in a bun, is getting thin; I can see her scalp underneath. She nods, stands up, takes a sharp knife from the block and passes it to me without a word. And so I cook my first ever soup. I've often watched Frieda, and now I do what she does. I spoon some clarified butter from the large pot and put it in the pan. Then I sweat the onions, garlic and two bay leaves. After that I add the rest of the vegetables — carrots, potatoes, celery, kohlrabi — then the meat stock, salt, pepper and some herbs. There are crusts of bread on the table, which we'll dunk in the soup later. Siegfried will want some meat with his soup, so I cut the leftovers of the roast beef into small pieces and add them just before the soup is ready. It actually tastes like the soup we usually have; I'm so proud of myself.

Siegfried doesn't seem to have noticed; he eats his soup just like he always does: thoughtfully and elegantly. 'Hands on the table!' Marianne says, turning to me. My hand was resting on my leg. When we're finished, she whispers, 'Say thank you to Frieda.' Unable to suppress a smile, I say politely, 'Thank you, Frieda, for that delicious soup.' She looks at me quizzically and says, 'Why's she thanking me when she cooked it herself?' Now Siegfried looks at me directly, grins and nods his head in approval.

'Oh,' Marianne says loudly, 'so now she's starting to do some real cooking. Well, that's useful at least.'

★   ★   ★

Early that afternoon Johannes comes home from school. These are his last few days; his leaving certificate is practically in the bag. In both our rooms upstairs, books are scattered all over the place. He's been studying hard.

The final summer of his schooldays is approaching. No-one knows what's going to happen after that — there are all sorts of opportunities now.

He takes my hands and pulls me onto the bed. 'Come on!' he says. 'It's hot up here. Take your dress off.' I do exactly as he says. The window is wide open, outside the birds are chirping, as if drunk with the joys of summer. I can't see any spiders, they don't come out to spin their fine threads until evening. Johannes puts his hand over my mouth; nobody must hear us. Nobody must know what love sounds like.

★　★　★

Two weeks have passed. It's July and we've got Western money. Not a drop of rain has fallen, the first hay has been harvested, Johannes has passed his leaving certificate with good grades. As a reward his parents, grandparents on his mother's side and Frieda gave him money. Frieda the most. We decide to go to Munich: my second trip to the West.

I have unhappy memories of the first. Queuing to get our 'welcome money' was a degrading experience, and I felt humiliated by the looks I got from a greengrocer when I asked him what this or that vegetable was called, and how I should cook it. Before that we'd been stuck for ages at the border, freezing cold. The first snow had fallen — early snow — and we weren't prepared for the hundreds of cars all wanting to get across the border. We waited for hours in our ice-cold car, just to get the money and finally see the West with our own eyes. I was disappointed. The reality of a freezing November day with rain and snow could not match the expectations I'd been building up all my life. The only shop I went into was that greengrocer's, and he was so unfriendly. Where we came from was written on our faces.

Now this second time, in summer. The old Wartburg groans from the effort of our unusually long drive, but when we cross into the West the roads improve at once. At the border we showed our I.D. cards and were waved through. It's still so hard to believe. We just kept on driving.

We're overtaken by everything on the motorway, even the large lorries. We smoke with the windows down and we feel like gods. After almost six hours in the car we get to Munich. I don't have any money, and even if I did I wouldn't know what to buy. They've got everything here, and I'd never be able to decide. Johannes, however, has a plan. We walk for a while, go past some shops and into others like everyone else, come out again and walk on. He holds my hand too tightly; I break free and look, look, look. The sounds and smells of the West are different.

He leaves me at a pavement café while he goes 'to get something'. Before he leaves he orders me a coffee with astounding confidence. I wonder what it is he needs to get here. But in fact I'm not much bothered. Just sitting here, watching, drinking my coffee and eating an unbelievably delicious slice of cake is more than I can cope with. I stare at people. It's so different here, so self-confident, so assured, so hard to describe. I've finished my coffee, I order another and a glass of wine as well. I'm holding a tiny notebook. I'd planned to write down the things I saw that were new to me, things I'd sometimes longed for. And now I realise that everything is new to me, I'd have to write it all down: the smell of the shops, the cleanliness of the streets, the bright façades of the houses, women's fashion, the excellent coffee, the beauty of the women here, their shaved legs and armpits, their soft, smooth skin, the men's flirtatious looks, the turquoise-coloured River Isar and the lightness of it all. And these amazing colours everywhere! I don't write down anything and suddenly my heart feels heavy. I want Johannes to come now and take me home. Now. My enthusiasm turns to utter despondency in a flash. I feel poor, ugly, lonely. I'm wearing a pretty dress too, but there's something about me. I don't know what it is, but it's different; I can't really explain. I can't enjoy anything here anymore; I'm quivering with anxiety as I wait for Johannes. Suddenly I'm plagued by the thought that he might not come back, he might not find me again. What would I do? I whisper to myself, 'Come on, Johannes, come back, come back now, please . . . ' At the next table a couple are grinning and looking over at me. In the stream of people passing by I'm looking for only one face. I gulp awkwardly from the bulbous glass, red wine drips onto my pale dress and I'm ashamed of everything about me.

Finally, finally I catch sight of Johannes; he's holding a white plastic bag.

Beaming with joy — I find this totally inappropriate — he sits beside me and orders himself a glass of wine. He drinks it quickly and doesn't stop kissing me.

'What took you so long?' I reproach him.

'You'll see,' he whispers with a smile. 'A surprise. We'll unpack it at home.' He's being very secretive.

When the bill arrives we can scarcely

believe our eyes: 21.50 D-Mark. A fortune, but nothing in comparison to what Johannes has just spent.

Then we drive home; there's nothing more for us to do here. Home — how lovely that sounds. We don't get back until late at night, all the lights are out, and all we can hear is an owl's screeching. Johannes fetches a dusty bottle of wine from the cellar and I glug it as if I'm dying of thirst, but I want more. 'Johannes,' I say, 'go and get another bottle.'

'I can't: Dad will notice. Then there'll be trouble.'

'I'll take the blame,' I say, not bothered, and off he goes. We've disturbed the spiders; they climb up again, swinging on their threads as they go. I stagger over to the sofa and let myself fall backwards. My dress rides up. Johannes unpacks his surprise. He beckons me over, I reel across the room feeling pleasantly light-headed. It's a camera, really a very, very good camera, as he keeps assuring me when I look at the receipt in disbelief: 1,980 D-Mark, and it's not even new.

'We can go anywhere now, there's no border any more,' he says, screwing on the lens. 'I'm going to take photos of everything, especially you.'

4

Today I'm going to see my mother. It's about a forty-minute walk. You start by following the road and then cut across fields. We live in one of the larger villages, with about five hundred inhabitants. With houses scattered all over the place and no proper centre, it's not half as pretty as the Brendels' village. There are only three farms left, and now on the edge of the village there are several modern blocks with very posh apartments, as Grandma Traudel likes to call them. Mum and I don't agree with her: the apartments are small, you don't have your own garden and you can hear it every time the neighbours cough.

We live in the old part of the village. Our house, painted reddish brown, is in a nice position, with the village pond directly opposite. Alongside the house runs a narrow alley lined with fruit trees, which we spent hours playing in as children. It might not be the oldest house in the village, but it's by far the most old-fashioned. Grandpa Lorenz has refused to modernise it in any way; we don't even have a flush loo. I don't know why he's been so stubborn, but Grandma Traudel says it's his way of punishing her for the reproachful looks she's given him while going on and on about the new developments.

You can see the baker's and the tavern from our house, while in the new part of the village there's a large co-op, the council offices with a small library, a kindergarten and the primary school, which has its own garden. We used to grow vegetables there, and in the summer months we even supplied the school kitchen.

From our garden you can see the church and the parsonage. The pastor ministers not only to our village, but to the other parishes in the area too. He doesn't have much to do; few people apart from the elderly go to church any more. I was friends with some of the pastor's seven children. I remember how much I enjoyed saying grace before dinner, when the whole family chorused, 'The eyes of all wait upon thee; and thou givest them their meat in due season. Thou openest thine hand, and satisfiest the desire of every living thing.' By contrast those lonely meals at home with my mother, where we never said grace and often didn't even speak, made me miserable.

You can't see our garden from the alley. It's quite large, with two cherry trees, an apple and a pear, a few currant bushes, raspberry canes and strawberry beds, some rows of lettuce, carrots, onions and potatoes, herb beds with parsley, chives and dill, a rabbit hutch and a chicken shed.

When I arrive my mother is reading in a deckchair beneath the apple tree. She looks terribly thin. I'm mortified by her skinny legs, which stick out from beneath her dress like stalks. She's the only one around here who owns any books. *Effi Briest* and *Anna Karenina* are still her absolute favourites. I've spent many wonderful hours with these books too, lost in daydreams and feeling the characters' suffering.

Grandma Traudel disapproved of all this — she only reads the newspaper — but she got used to it over time. My mother inherited her love of reading from her own parents, Sigrun and Hanno. Sigrun came from the Hamburg bourgeoisie, but two years after the war, when she was eighteen, she fell in love with a communist, Hanno Breede. She followed him to the northern part of the Soviet Occupation Zone. They found a house on the moors there and settled down. This was a blow for Sigrun's family — they'd never really liked Hanno. But Sigrun and Hanno had five children: Ernst, Wilhelm, Hannah, Torben and Walther. My mother was the middle child and the only girl. The eldest and youngest sons died: Ernst just after he was born, and Walther fell out of a window when he was four. It wasn't so high up, only three and a half metres, but the boy died on impact. Hanno worked as a newspaper editor in the local town, and later ran the local agricultural collective.

'Oh, so you've come back then,' she says, standing up. 'Tell me, how's life at the Brendels'? And how are you?' She tilts her head to one side. 'Are you still going to school? You left your maths and physics books here.'

I'm not even going to attempt to lie, but I don't want to alarm her more than necessary, so I say, 'Life's good at the Brendels', they treat me like their own daughter . . . but I don't go to school much . . . they're not too happy about that.' She looks at me, imploring, waiting for me to go on, and I say, 'I don't know, Mum . . . maybe I won't do my leaving certificate, maybe instead I'll look for an apprenticeship or help out on the farm. I don't know yet. I don't think I'm going to finish school.'

She looks at me sadly. She has invested her hopes in me, but I can't fulfil them. All she says is 'Oh,' and after a long pause, 'We'll have to send off some applications then. The new academic year starts in September — that's just around the corner.'

I don't know what to say. I was expecting her to hit the roof and force me to go back to school. In fact that's probably what I wanted her to do. She's the mother, after all. And I'm the child.

But she falls silent, and I say faintly, 'Have you heard from Dad?'

'Ye-es,' she says, her voice rising as she draws out the word to a second syllable. 'He's getting married again.'

'What? When?' I ask in horror, but I'm happy that the subject has changed to something that diverts the attention from me.

'Her name's Nastja and she's from Leningrad. But they're going to live near here. And I think she's already pregnant.' I feel myself tingling all over. 'She's nineteen, by the way,' my mother adds, pursing her lips.

'Maybe we'll be friends, then,' I say as dispassionately as I can. But she appears not to have heard me. She's had her hair cut, and she looks tired. The factory where she'd had an office job for almost ten years closed last week. But I don't understand why she had to have her hair cut. It was so beautiful, thick and slightly wavy, much more beautiful than my own.

'We need to have a proper talk some time,

Maria,' she now says sternly, even though her reedy voice suggests otherwise. 'You know I lost my job, and I don't have any prospects of finding another one. I don't know what the future holds. Somehow, of course, life goes on, but I haven't a clue what we're going to live off.' She picks at her fingernails. 'Ah, well,' she says, 'I've still got a little money put aside — from the sale of the house. But your father doesn't pay any maintenance for you and, to be honest, I'd rather you learned a profession. Staying put with the Brendels is crazy, don't you think?'

We're facing each other, but she's not looking at me. Her feet are bare and I feel sorry for her. I'd like to give her an answer, give her a solution, I even feel obliged to have a plan; it was my decision to move out after all — at sixteen! You don't just leave home at sixteen without any idea what you're going to do, but I have no idea. I feel utterly empty.

Now she looks at me, with that particular expression which asks: Maybe you can help me out too, what should I do? Tell me, Maria!

But I don't even know myself, Mum. Can't you understand that?

This is the way it always is: there will be no decision unless I make it myself.

Such emptiness —

I go into the house, climb the stairs to my

attic room, this ancient room with its nineteenth-century cupboards and bed, its saggy mattress in three sections. Above the bed hangs a Symbolist picture called 'Nymphs and Saturn', and I've often dreamed I was in it. The nymph in the middle wears a blue hairband, and her face is most clearly visible. She's supposed to look like my mother did when she was a girl. The picture came from her father, and it's right for her.

★ ★ ★

You can't see my desk beneath the gable window as it's buried under mountains of books and notes. I hurriedly gather a few things together — pens, a pad, a few old passport photos, a book — grab some clothes from my wardrobe, and chuck everything into a suitcase. I'm going to have to find work, I think; I don't have any money.

Then I put the case down, it's too heavy to carry back all that way. I run down the stairs, past my mother's two small rooms and the tiny room where my great-grandmother Milda sleeps. She spends her days packing leftover food into small plastic bags and stashing it in cupboards, where it can rot away in peace. I pass my grandparents' apartment in the basement and go through the back door into the garden. My mother is still standing like a statue beneath the apple tree. I give her a fleeting but firm embrace and promise to come back soon. Then out into the alley, out of the village, away, away, away, just away. I feel calmer when the village is out of sight.

★   ★   ★

On the walk back I cut across the cornfield. The young plants come up to my knees; the harvest won't be for a good couple of months yet. I rarely come this way, it passes Henner's farm, which means past the dogs and horses so wild only Henner can ride them. When he's on good form he looks like a landowner from another era, tearing across the pasture at a gallop, his dogs running beside him. He not a man of the modern age, more like someone who's been born in the wrong century. Marianne says he's in better shape, he must have stopped drinking. No-one seriously believes that, but when he was last in the shop he was stone-cold sober.

The corn tickles my legs, my dress catches on the leaves. I brush the plants with my hands, which feel quite numb after my visit to my mother.

In the distance I can see Henner. He's in the paddock, wearing old riding boots, narrow brown trousers and a filthy shirt which must once have been white. The dogs are lazing in the shade of an apple tree. Marianne told me that they even killed one of his foals last year. He beat the dogs with a stick until they howled.

I walk slowly, thinking about my mother; she looked so sad. What will become of her without my father, without a job and having to live with her parents-in-law? It was her sadness that drove me from the house. It drains every scrap of energy from my body, and the joy from my heart.

Henner truly is a handsome man. I realised that when he was in the shop: a hulking body that moves powerfully, but with fine facial features. He has deep-set, expressive eyes surrounded by small, dark lines, and a hint of bitterness around his mouth, although when he smiles it disappears completely. You can't tell that he's a drinker.

Suddenly he turns round. The dogs leap up as if obeying a command, and in a few bounds they're at the paddock fence. 'Henner!' I scream, 'Get them away!' He laughs, throwing back his head.

'They don't like skinny girls!' he shouts back at me, but whistles to them all the same.

My legs are trembling. I feel queer, as Marianne would say, and collapse in a heap.

Tears flood my eyes. I don't know what's happening to me; I sob and sob, burying my face in my arms. I only snap out of it when I feel Henner's hands, and his heady, sour male scent envelops me. He strokes my head — I'd never have thought he could be so tender — and slowly pulls me up. I don't dare open my eyes, and he whispers soothingly to me, 'It's alright, Maria, nothing happened. It's alright, I'll take you back to the farm.' I can barely walk, his arm is around me and his hand brushes my breast: it feels like it's burning. I stop. 'Shhh,' he says, gripping my arm. In a single, fluid stroke his hand moves down my neck, across my breasts, tummy, to my inner thigh, then up a little. I wrestle free and run, but he soon catches me again, and this time he looks at me quite differently.

'I'm sorry,' he says. 'I didn't mean to frighten you, I'm really sorry. Don't say a word to anyone, Maria. Do you hear me?' Holding me with his outstretched arm he goes on talking softly: 'Nothing happened, did it? Nothing at all!' I nod silently, he lets go of me, and I walk away without turning round.

★ ★ ★

There is a commotion at the farm. Siegfried has discovered some thin, transparent tubing beneath the steering wheel of the Wartburg. He followed the tube to its origin and found a plastic container of vodka under the bonnet. Only one person could have put it there. When I walk into the yard I see Siegfried and Alfred standing by the door: Alfred with his head bowed; Siegfried gesticulating wildly. I creep past them — they don't even notice I'm there — go upstairs to the attic and get into bed with *The Brothers Karamazov*. Zossima has died, but not before sharing the wisdom of a lifetime with his fellow monks: 'Brothers, have no fear of men's sin. Love a man even in his sin, for that is the semblance of Divine Love and is the highest love on earth.'

And then that incredible thing happens: Zossima's body decomposes on the very day he dies!

★ ★ ★

At teatime we all gather in the garden. There's cake with fresh strawberries, coffee and water. Marianne asks me how my visit to my mother went. But when I try to formulate a reply I burst out laughing, shocking everyone at the table. Siegfried gives me a serious glance, and holding back the tears I try to explain what Madame Khokhlakov said about Zossima: that she hadn't expected such behaviour. Such behaviour! I'm practically falling about with laughter. As if Zossima decomposed of his own will, as if he'd told himself, 'I know, I'll play a trick on them. I'll just decompose right now instead of taking a few days — or not at all, like some saints.' The parents exchange glances; Frieda acts as if nothing's happening. Nobody else is laughing.

Johannes grins as best he can with a mouth full of strawberry cake. In his lap is his camera, he hasn't been able to put it down for days. The family was horrified when they heard how much he'd paid for it; he could have bought a car with that money. Frieda wanted him to go travelling; he ought to go to Greece, she said; it's meant to be stunning, sheer paradise. Those were her words: sheer pa-ra-dise. There had been a travel programme on the television about Santorini. Now that they can go wherever they like, he should have gone to Greece — he could even have flown there. Yes, that's what the boy should have done with the money. But Johannes has other plans. Up in the attic there is a small room without any windows. And in this room Johannes has a secret. In a minute he'll show me what it is.

We wolf down our cake, quickly swallowing a second piece, and then go up. Such excitement. At first I can't see anything; it's pitch black in the room, unbearably hot, and it reeks of chemicals. Johannes leads me to a chair, then turns on the light.

Along the wall in front of me is a worktop, and on it a large, mysterious contraption and several shallow plastic trays containing liquid, as well as bottles labelled 'Developer' and 'Fixer', and some boxes of photographic paper. Above this hangs a washing line with pegged-up photographs, and I am in every one of them: asleep in bed in the morning, brushing my teeth naked, bent over *The Brothers Karamazov*, lying in the garden in the sun, leaning against the old shed by the weir — naked again, my hair in a plait. Johannes smiles and says, 'Now I know what I want to do: I'm going to study art, we're going to get away from here.' He gives me a piercing look. 'Dad wants me to take over the farm. Now that we're allowed to own the land again, he says, we might be able to make some money. But I need to get away.' I feel dizzy, I don't know what to say, he looks so happy. But what about me? I've only just got here. He goes on and on, without saying very much: 'Do you know what? I'd have done what Hartmut did, I'd have applied to leave, and just like Hartmut I wouldn't have said a word to anyone. But now we can go wherever we like, we can do what we like.' He swings his right hand through the air emphatically. 'You would have been barred from going to college, Maria,' he continues. 'You didn't go through the state initiation ceremony. But you've still got to finish school. We'll wait until then; it's too late for me to start this semester anyway. I'll go on working for Dad for a while, and then we'll be off.' His eyes are bulging with happiness about his future prospects. Then I think of Henner and feel the place where he touched my breast. It's burning. Johannes kneels on the floor in front of me and puts his head in my lap. 'Oh, Maria . . . ' he says, 'we're going to have such a different life from the one we'd imagined.' It's only then that I notice the pictures on the wall. Five of them, in small black frames. Five children. Three girls, two boys, lying down with their eyes closed. Because they're all dead.

5

The house is abuzz with excitement. It's the third week in July. The visit is imminent. You can't communicate with Frieda; the usual order in the kitchen has given way to chaos. Baking, cooking, cleaning. Now the entire village knows: tomorrow the Westerners are coming!

Frieda and I are bent over a mountain of leavened dough; she shows me what it should feel like when it's just right: like the soft breast of a woman. I feel my own breast to compare; Frieda lets out a hearty laugh. There's definitely a certain similarity in the consistency. We're making *gugelhupf* and fruitcake — I can do it in my sleep these days — and for lunch we're going to have vegetable soup with semolina dumplings, followed by roast beef with potato dumplings and red cabbage, and a sabayon with real vanilla for pudding. Henner got us the real vanilla. He was over in the West yesterday and brought us back a few presents, because Marianne is always generous towards him. When he has been feeling down she has occasionally given him something: a chicken, or a few onions and vegetables. So he's very much in her debt. He brought me something too: a bag of caramels and a butterfly hairclip inlaid with ruby-red stones. This earned me a suspicious glance from Marianne. Henner's much better, they say. There's a chance farmers will get back the land that once belonged to their parents. At least that's what Siegfried is hoping. No-one knows any details at this stage. In the G.D.R., the Brendels were one of the few families that were not collective farmers. Henner, on the other hand, worked for years in the agricultural collective before giving it up to be at the farm because the rest of his family had died. And that probably suited him fine.

After expropriation Heinrich and Frieda were allowed to keep three-quarters of a hectare. That was a lot by G.D.R. standards, and yet they had to reduce their livestock holding, which now wasn't enough to live off, so Siegfried came up with the idea of the sawmill. The rest of the land, forty hectares at least, went to the collective. The large hay meadows down by the river were only the Brendels' on lease. The same happened to Henner's family.

I've heard he's been clearing up a bit at the farm. The dogs are quiet at the moment, the horses clean and well groomed. I can go for a ride if I like, he said, with Johannes of course, but I don't trust his horses.

Frieda releases me from the kitchen for an hour, so Johannes and I go to the river. Until only a few weeks ago the water here would look different every day: green, blue, yellow, rust-red, and it stank of rotten eggs. That was because of the chemical factory upstream, where my mother worked. Now on hot days the cattle go to the riverbank and drink their fill.

★　★　★

I have discovered why Zossima prostrated himself before Dmitry. Shortly before his death he said to Alexey, 'I bowed down yesterday to the great suffering in store for him.' Alexey was beside himself with worry.

★　★　★

We're sitting by the river with our feet in the water. Johannes only ever sees me through the camera lens these days. Every gesture becomes a picture, every look becomes infinity. He delivers me from time and captures a moment, which is then immediately lost for ever — every picture is a small death.

Later we wander through the meadow as

far as the railway tracks. We walk along the tracks until we reach a bridge. It crosses the river diagonally and is about fifty metres long. To get to the other side you have to walk down the middle of the tracks, on the rotten sleepers; there's barely any space to either side. We put our heads on the tracks to listen out for any humming and check for slight vibrations indicating an oncoming train. No humming. We can't see any track workers either. You can't escape a train by jumping into the river; it's too shallow at this point, and full of large stones. But over there, on the other side, there are the prettiest wild flowers and a spot that no-one else knows about. When we reach it I undress and paddle in the river. Johannes shouts something at me; he's tinkering with his camera. I shout back that he should join me, it's lovely in the water, but he doesn't hear me.

We don't get home until evening. Frieda's grumbling, wondering where I've been all this time. 'I could have done with her help,' she says. Then she smiles and says, 'Why doesn't she just go and fetch me some chives from the garden?' I dash out.

For dinner there's black bread with butter, thin slices of hard-boiled egg sprinkled with chives, and salad with a dressing of oil, vinegar, water and sugar. Dressing is a word we've learned only recently. Siegfried gets a fried schnitzel as well. We're sitting at the table in the yard, amongst the flower tubs, when Siegfried says that he's really looking forward to seeing Hartmut. He would have been quite happy to disappear back then too; he only stayed because it would have broken his mother's heart. That's how he puts it. Frieda doesn't stir. Marianne looks from one to the other. Perhaps she's wondering what to say, but in the end decides it would be better to keep quiet. They'll be here tomorrow, the Westerners, from Rosenheim, from Bavaria.

I decide I will go back to my mother's after all, to fetch my suitcase. In it are some clothes I'd like to wear when our visitors are here. I've heard that they make fun of us over there; 'I can't get that magazine cover out of my head; the one with the picture of a girl holding a cucumber and saying 'my first banana'. It's still a lovely, bright summer's evening, but there's a distinct chill drifting up from the river. I borrow a scarf from Marianne, tell Johannes I might be back late, and set off.

* * *

When I get there, my grandparents are sitting on the bench outside the house. I stop to talk, but I don't go into any detail. Then I ask about my father, Ulrich, the eldest of their four sons. So it's true, he is going to marry this Nastja, a nineteen-year-old. My grandmother asks whether I'm going to move back in, now that the house is being renovated. 'We're even getting a flush toilet,' she says. And the old washhouse is being converted into a tool shed. My grandmother used to do the laundry there once a week. It was so hot that the steam rose to the ceiling in huge clouds before dripping back down. The laundry tub was almost the size of my grandmother. She would stir the washing with a long wooden paddle, first to the left, then to the right, until it was clean. The dirtiest items were scrubbed on the wash-board.

Mum is going to have her own bathroom with a shower. The old boiler and the tub where we'd have a bath every Friday, one after the other, are being ripped out. The small room behind my grandparents' kitchen is going to be a guest room. It's awkward for all of them that Mum's still living here. We had our own house for a few years, over in the new part of the village. I was ten when we moved in, and before then we'd lived with my grandparents. I had a lovely, bright room on the second floor, a fold-down bed, blue-and-white checked curtains and lilac wallpaper with a flower pattern. The living room had an open hearth where we'd light a fire every day around Christmas time. It was a brand-new house and Dad had built it himself.

After the divorce, when Dad disappeared to the Soviet Union for good, we stayed on there. I was thirteen, Mum thirty-three. But six months later we packed our things into boxes and Grandma got our old rooms ready again. We couldn't keep the house on without Dad's income. My mother sold it.

I chose the attic bedroom at my grandparents'. I was on my own up there; the other rooms were full of old furniture and junk, no-one slept in them. I had a chamber pot under my bed again, because it was a long, cold walk to the outside loo. The night's deposits were tipped out in the morning, and Grandma would rinse the chamber pots with hot water.

This backwards move didn't particularly bother me. But Mum suffered terribly.

I can hear her steps — such tiny, delicate, careful steps, as if she's creeping about. But she always walks like that. She's brought my case down. The weight of it pulls her over to one side; she drops it beside me. My grandparents ask me to pass on their greetings to Frieda; say hello from Traudel and Lorenz, they reiterate, as if I didn't know their names. Mum gives me a nod that she's ready to leave. I feel more cheerful.

Mum brings the Trabant out of the garage. Dad left it behind; he couldn't drive it all those thousands of kilometres to the Soviet Union; that would have been too much for an old car. The tank is almost empty, but there'll be enough to get us to the farm — it's downhill practically all the way. I sit in the passenger seat beside Mum, wedge the suitcase between my knees, and quickly crank the window down. I don't know why, but I feel a slight chill.

A few hundred metres before the Brendels' farm Mum turns off the engine and lets the car freewheel. She's trying to save petrol, seeing as it's all downhill from here. I watch as she removes the key from the ignition. That's odd.

To the left of the road there's an embankment; to the right, meadows and woodland extend down into the valley. All of a sudden I hear a click. The steering wheel locks. At this point the road bends round to the right, but the car keeps going straight. I grab onto Mum's arm and she looks at me, her eyes wide with fright as the Trabant climbs the embankment, slowly, very slowly, veers right, tips onto its side, and finally, as if in slow motion, rolls onto the roof. We're not strapped in so we fall, noiselessly, first sideways, then onto our heads, and end up lying there stiff with shock. For a few seconds there's silence. I can't even hear her breathing.

I'm the first to try to open the door, but after several futile attempts I climb out through the window. My mother follows me. She still hasn't said a word.

And then we're sitting there trembling by the side of the road, next to an upturned, sky-blue Trabant. In Mum's hand is the key, which for some unfathomable reason she'd taken out of the ignition. Yes, she actually did. She says nothing. I say nothing. I feel ashamed for her. I don't know how long we've been sitting there — it can't be more than a few minutes — but it feels like an eternity. Suddenly I hear dogs behind us. Their barking brings me out of my stupor and back into the present. It's Henner coming from the woods. He has a sack over his shoulder and I find myself wondering what's in it. He must be hiding something. Seeing us sitting there he approaches, looks at the car and shakes his head. 'We'll get that back the right way up,' he says. My mind is now empty. I watch Henner put down the sack and I don't let it out of my sight. He's talking to my mother, and now she's shaking her head. But then she stands up, both of them lift the car in one single movement — all the power coming from Henner, no doubt — and set it back on its four wheels. My mother takes out the suitcase, puts it down by my feet — just like that, without even looking at me — then gets into the car and drives off.

★ ★ ★

Later I'd sometimes say that everything that happened must have been because of the shock. Some things, for sure, but not everything.

I pick up the case and start walking. Henner slings the sack back over his shoulder. With large strides he catches up with me, takes the suitcase and says, 'Come with me!' His house is not far. We turn right onto the path and walk to the farm in silence. The dogs jump up at me, and I let them; I'm looking at the sack, but there's nothing moving inside it. I follow him into the house, into the kitchen. He puts the case onto a chair and drops the sack by the cooker. Wood, I tell myself, it's just wood, but why does he need to heat the place? It's summer. He pushes me towards the table, sits me on a chair with armrests, shakes his head and says, 'That was something else.' Beside me is a glass with clear liquid. I pick it up and drink — vodka. Henner takes the scarf from my shoulders. His big dogs are scratching at the door. He's shut them out. He doesn't want witnesses, I think, they could bark it to the whole world. I like this image so much that I almost burst out laughing. Something in the sack moves, it can't be wood after all. Standing behind me he puts his hands around my neck. I'm going to die. If I don't die now I'll never be afraid again. The dogs are making a racket, I have another sip. He lets me go again and I finish my drink. Now I can see my bare feet. I don't have my shoes on any more; Henner has them in his hands and he tosses them carelessly into the corner by the sack. I'm not mistaken: something *is* moving inside. 'Now I've caught you,' he jokes, 'and dragged you back to my den.' Then he laughs, and it sounds to me like the rumble of thunder.

A hare, I think, there's a hare in the sack. He's set a trap and caught a hare. For the dogs, those beasts of his.

I don't know how he got me into the other room. Perhaps I just followed him. There's an open window, a yellowed curtain is billowing in the evening breeze. Between the lime trees I can see the gable of the Brendels' farmhouse and the light on in the window.

Johannes is waiting for me. My dress has a side zip, my fingertips are touching the top of the window frame, small pieces of paint flake off, and Henner's hands are rough. Like a sleepwalker I step out of my knickers and dress, which is now covering my feet. He's breathing gently and rhythmically on my neck, and I'm sure my heart is about to stop. It misses a beat, then sparks back into life: a shudder flashes through my body, an uncontrollable shudder, and then several more. He holds me firmly until it stops. I can feel small stones beneath my feet; the dogs have quietened down. From behind his hands press against my pelvic bone and inch downwards to my inner thighs. Then, with gentle force, he pushes my legs apart. I support myself on the windowsill so I don't fall over. Zossima springs to mind as he quotes from St John's Gospel, saying to Alexey, 'Except a corn of wheat fall into the ground and die, it abideth alone: but if it die, it bringeth forth much fruit.'

Then I fall onto the bed and into a deep ecstasy.

I don't deny him anything, not even when he lifts me from the bed and says I must kneel. Not even when he wraps my plait around his hand and watches me from above, doing what he tells me to. Now it's him trembling. I'm going to be seventeen soon. In the old days that made you a woman. My grandmother had her first child at seventeen, that's what it used to be like.

But still, I can't help shedding a few tears. He lifts me up and sits me on the edge of the bed. I fall back, close my eyes, and feel the warm humidity of his breath between my legs, then his lips, his tongue — I'm falling. He makes a noise like a dying animal — a furious, desperate panting. I don't dare to open my eyes. He grabs my legs, pushes them wide open, and enters me. He starts thrusting, then faster and harder. I slide backwards, he grips my arms, turns me onto my stomach and pushes a pillow under my pelvis. I don't understand, I try to turn over, I want to see his face, but he puts his heavy hand on my neck and holds me down. I close my eyes.

★ ★ ★

Shortly before midnight I leave Henner's house carrying my case. As a goodbye he takes my head in his hands and plants a kiss on my forehead. Then he puts his index finger to his lips. I nod, perhaps not distinctly enough; I sense that his eyes on my back lack their usual certainty. So I turn and repeat the gesture he was looking for.

6

The following morning I get up before Johannes. He was asleep when I got back; he probably thought I was spending the night at my mother's.

I'd lain down beside him fully clothed. Shivering, sweating. My sweat mingled with Henner's odour; the cracked patches of his dried semen felt taut on my skin. I was terrified that Johannes might wake up, stroke me and realise what had happened; but I couldn't bring myself to wash off the smell. I closed my eyes and took a deep breath.

I couldn't sleep.

Nor can I forget.

And now the morning sun with its revealing light. I creep out of the room and downstairs to the bathroom where I fill the tub. Marianne is in the shop, Siegfried out in the animal sheds, and Frieda is standing at the gate waiting for the guests. It's just gone eight o'clock; they won't be here before noon. When I undress I see the bruises on my body. I feel desperate. What have I done? What did Henner do? Everyone's going to notice, starting with Johannes, of course. How can I hide the traces of his hands all over my neck, arms and thighs? There's no denying it, it can't be explained away. They'll send me back to my mother and the shame will stick to me like bad luck. That's how it still is in our village, even though it's 1990.

Outside clouds are looming; it's going to rain. The air is cooling, a wind is picking up. The weather will save me! From my suitcase I take a blue dress with mid-length sleeves, blue with white spots; it covers my knees. Over it I wear a white cardigan and I wrap a scarf around my neck. My face doesn't give anything away; he spared that.

Right at the bottom of my case is an envelope; I didn't put it there. It's not sealed, and there's a note inside with the single sentence: 'He lay awake at night, desiring her, and he had her.' I look over at Johannes, who's still asleep and knows nothing. I'm utterly ashamed, and yet — I keep the note.

Later, at elevenses, I start talking. I babble on and on at Johannes. About my grandparents, how they're renovating the house after all these years, about how Traudel was always so envious of people who had automatic washing machines while she was still using a tub. I blather about my mother and how she's out of work, about my father and his young Russian girl, who I might make friends with, but perhaps I'll hate her, if she's pretty I'll definitely hate her, and she's supposed to be very pretty, Grandpa saw a photo and said, 'not bad', Grandpa knows all about pretty girls, he had an eye for the women, as the landlord of the local tavern once put it, but that's all in the past, I mean he's an old man now. Johannes only looks up when I'm talking about the Russian girl, and says, 'She's just a year older than me.'

I nod and continue my monologue. Eventually Siegfried comes into the kitchen and says they must be here soon, the Westerners. 'Yes,' I say. 'It can't be long now!'

And it isn't long, which is a relief, because Frieda's had butterflies for hours. She's quite distracted. She was in the kitchen cooking at four this morning. Everything was done by the time I came down for breakfast; lunch only needs warming up. After a while we hear a soft purring in the drive — a completely new sound to us. Lukas in particular will remember it for a long time. He's never seen a car like it: a real Mercedes, we hadn't expected that. Frieda steps aside and peers into the distance as if she were expecting more visitors. But then she closes the gate and, head bowed, approaches Hartmut, who has just got out of the car. She clasps her hands over her large tummy, nodding all the while. 'Is that you?' she asks, nodding a few more times.

Hartmut is unmistakably Siegfried's brother. Not that he's a carbon copy, but it's the movements, gestures, the way he raises his head, the fleeting grins. Like Siegfried he has a large head and bright, wide-apart eyes with thick blond eyelashes, but his nose is narrower and his lips aren't as full. He looks pale in comparison to Siegfried, whose skin is brown and leathery from his daily work on the farm and in the fields, from the biting winter wind and burning summer sun. The brothers greet each other with a firm handshake. Marianne is in tears and throws her arms around Hartmut. She's made herself look lovely, has Marianne. She's wearing a wide black skirt printed with lavish roses, and a tight-fitting, low-cut red top.

Then the wife gets out of the car. I've been watching her. She had flipped down the sun visor, which must have a mirror in it, put on some lipstick and smoothed her eyebrows. Now she makes straight for Frieda, offers her hand and says, 'I'm Gisela. Delighted to meet you, after all these years.'

'You're telling me,' Frieda says, without really looking at her. Gisela is wearing a grey trouser suit and a white blouse. Her blonde hair is tied up. She's quite elegant. Her shoes are black, and they don't have heels; she's almost as tall as Hartmut, and therefore Siegfried too. Although Marianne's wearing high heels — and she often wears them, even in the animal sheds — she only comes up to Gisela's nose. Then the rest of us greet each other in turn, offering our hands and introducing ourselves. We all look through the gleaming car windows at the back seat, where the children are asleep. They are seven and nine; Hartmut took his time to have children.

Frieda hurries into the kitchen to warm up the food while the rest of us stay outside. Marianne has linked arms with Gisela and is showing her the farmyard; Siegfried and Lukas are gawping into the open bonnet of the Mercedes. Johannes follows Hartmut, who looks as if he's about to cry. I can understand why. Alfred slinks around for a while, then goes back to his work.

No-one take any notice of me, and Johannes has not commented on what I'm wearing: the scarf around my neck and the cardigan — it may have cooled down a little, but it's still almost twenty degrees. I take advantage of the time before lunch and go for a walk with *The Brothers Karamazov*. So Alexey has gone to visit Grushenka after all, even though he must have been aware that her charms would be the ruin of him. But everything turned out differently.

I lie down in the grass behind the sawmill. The words dance on the page and blur.

Now, like a thief, sleep takes hold of me; it descends from the gloomy sky and sinks heavily onto my abused body, ill-treated by love. I can feel Henner's hands — coarse, gentle, brutal, expectant — and I long for them . . .

★ ★ ★

When I return the children are awake. They're running around the yard, shouting in their throaty dialect. I find it hard to understand them. Gisela is watching them from the kitchen window. Then she motions to us to come in for lunch. Hartmut is sitting beside Frieda, holding her hands in his. This moment belongs to them alone, a silent tableau that harbours all the suffering of a woman who thought she'd lost her son, and all the joy of their reunion. The kitchen feels too small, the rest of us are just intruding, how can we eat lunch now? Without a word I withdraw and go back up to the spiders' nest, my home.

Something inside me died last night.

I take the note Henner put in my case and write something on the other side. Then I return it to the envelope and run to his house as quickly as I can. The window from which I saw the Brendels' farm yesterday is still open. I throw the envelope inside.

But just then, as the envelope glides to the floor, I am overcome by terrible guilt. After making sure that no-one's around, I climb in through that same window and grab the envelope. Before I can leave again Henner opens the door. It's the first time I've seen him look surprised. He stops dead, looks at the window, then at me, and I realise at once that this is my one chance to escape. A life can be changed by a single moment. His gaze rests on the envelope in my hand, he flashes a smile, and I realise that my hesitation is fatal. He comes up to me, takes the envelope, opens it, pulls out the note and reads the following words aloud: ' . . . and he can have her again.'

★   ★   ★

No words can describe the dreadful feeling of shame which forces my eyes to the floor. I want the earth to swallow me whole. As I stand there he doesn't say anything. I don't know which is the strongest feeling: my urgent desire for another night like the last one, my present humiliation, fear, my girlish pride, or the wish to see this pride shattered.

I don't move a muscle.

He takes a step closer; he's been drinking again. As it hits me, his boozy breath sends my head spinning, making me feel slightly sick.

'So,' he says slowly, stroking his close-cropped hair. 'So, he can have her again, can he? Well.' He goes past me and closes the window. 'I see.' The dogs are sitting by the door. Even sitting they seem as big as I am. 'A haughty one, this girl,' Henner says. 'Granting him the favour of a final visit . . . What is she waiting for? Take those clothes off!' I look at him in disbelief, trying to understand what might have offended him, but I don't understand, not yet, and the dogs are guarding the door. He grabs the back of my head and pulls me towards him. Unwinding the scarf from my neck, he stops. He looks, opens his mouth, closes it again. His fingers touch the bruises he caused yesterday; his eyes ask whether anybody knows, whether Johannes knows, whether the police are about to turn up, what I'm going to do, whether I'll tell all, whether everything's out in the open now. Everything.

My shame subsides. I wait for him to say something. He's still looking at me, stroking my neck. His eyes are reddened from the schnapps. Maybe we're both thinking the same thing.

He's forty, I'm sixteen. Thorsten Henner

and Maria Bergmann. It was not rape, even though it looks like it. I'm the one in control now. But a man like Henner is not going to let himself be dominated by a sixteen-year-old girl.

This I realise straightaway. I try to catch his eye, which is now roving restlessly around the room. 'No, Henner, nobody knows, nobody. I swear,' I say to him. 'And I won't tell anybody either. I really won't.' He gives me a penetrating look, trying to read my thoughts, but he doesn't believe me. 'You have to promise me, Maria!' he says, gripping my shoulders. I nod quickly and say, 'Yes. Yes, I promise!'

He leaves the room and I'm standing there alone; but he comes back with some ointment. He rubs it on those areas on my neck, and then kisses them, the bruises, the marks that betray his guilt. And with every one of his caresses I feel as if I'm looking at myself through his eyes. A girl, dark-blonde with a long plait, not especially tall, slim, square-shouldered, serious face. Narrow nose, small mouth, but with full lips, large eyes, very bright and very green in the sunlight.

★   ★   ★

As I'm about to leave he asks me to wait. I wander through some of the ancient rooms, the dogs tail me mistrustfully; they're not used to having to share their master. I stop by a glass-fronted linen cupboard. Henner is behind me again, he slips me another note and puts his arm around me. The quietness in this house is greater than anywhere else. The dogs' growling, the creaking of floorboards, his heavy breath — I cannot hear anything else. There are sounds which have no connection with time. That's the way it is at Henner's house. I lean on him and he asks me, 'What are you reading at the moment? Marianne says you read a lot . . . '

'The Brothers Karamazov,' I say, rather proud that it happens to be this book.

'Who do you prefer, Katarina Ivanov or Grushenka?' he asks, and I say without hesitation, 'Grushenka.'

'Why Grushenka?'

'Because she's passionate. And honest. I don't believe that Katarina Ivanov loves Dmitry at all. She's a hypocrite.'

He laughs and says, 'That was a good answer, Maria. It's reassuring.'

★　★　★

The Brendels have been waiting for me. They've been sitting at the lunch table for ages, and when I come through the door

67

Frieda says, 'Where on earth did you get to? We've all been looking for you.' I take it as a sign that I properly belong here; they missed me; I mean something. It feels good. I mutter something about being tired and going for a walk, and only Alfred looks at me searchingly. Hartmut and Siegfried are deep in conversation. Hartmut has a lot to say, about how difficult it was in Bavaria to begin with, his studies, graduating as an engineer and his first job with a construction company, finally setting up his own planning office, and his marriage to Gisela, a teacher's daughter from Garmisch-Partenkirchen. He met her in a mountain hut while skiing, and they've been together for almost ten years. Their children were planned and Gisela doesn't have to work. Marianne is particularly interested by this; she had to put Johannes in a crèche when he was only eight weeks old, and she cried for days. This was normal, she was still working in town at the time. Marianne is not from the village. Siegfried met her at a dance in the county town. Both her parents worked at the collective paper factory, and Marianne did shift work there too.

By the time Lukas was born she had settled at the farm. It must have taken years for her to get used to farm life. Frieda had strongly advised Siegfried against marrying her. Town girls never became proper farmers, she said, even though she herself had married a teacher's son. Marianne didn't have much time with her second baby either, but at least he didn't have to go to a crèche. Frieda looked after the little one as best she could, and even Alfred helped out with the childcare sometimes. Deep down he's a good soul, Frieda likes to say. I'm not so sure.

To my left sits Johannes with his camera, to my right Alfred, his mouth full. He has a way of eating which I find utterly repulsive, but for some reason he's allowed to get away with everything, even eating with his mouth open and bending so far over his plate that his head almost touches the rim. Frieda says this makes the distance shorter, and so there's less spillage on the table. There's still much about the Brendel family that I don't understand.

Hartmut's efforts in the West paid off. He has an office with two employees, his own house, a garden, a Mercedes, a nice wife, even if she's a little sensitive — you can see this by the way Alfred's black fingernails put her off her lunch — and two healthy children, who are 'a little rough around the edges', as Marianne will say later. Frieda doesn't take her eyes off him and refills his plate the moment he empties it.

They're going to stay in Frieda's part of the

house, where there are six rooms: two for Alfred, the remaining four for Frieda. Plenty of space. For me this visit couldn't have come at a better time. It helps me hide my secret. That evening there's a violent storm; I sit at the window and look over at Henner's farm. It's pitch black over there.

7

The following morning the air is cooler and fresher than it's been for weeks, giving me every reason to wear the scarf around my neck. Johannes disappears into his darkroom straight after breakfast and doesn't even emerge for lunch. He's displaying an obsessiveness which makes us all wonder, especially Marianne. He's hung pictures of the farm beside those of the dead children. Johannes has photographed everything: Alfred mucking out the barn; Marianne feeding the chickens; Siegfried in the sawmill; the cattle on the pasture; the sheep; the geese; the chickens; Frieda down by the river, looking at the water; Frieda at the gate, looking along the road. And me over and over again.

We hardly talk any more, all I hear now is: 'The light is perfect, sit over there. No, no, no, not like that. Look to the right. No, Maria, with your eyes, not your head!' In fact Johannes doesn't see me any more, all he sees is pictures.

Until a few days ago I would have done anything to win back his attention. I'd have talked, charmed, ranted, whatever you do when your loved one turns his back on you. But I behave calmly; with apparent generosity I allow him to indulge in the magic of his new passion. I'm quite indifferent. My only real interest lies in the man on the neighbouring farm.

★   ★   ★

I wander through the yard, the note in my right hand. Alfred shuffles past me into the barn. There's a twinkle in his tiny eyes; his cheeks are sunken as he barely has any teeth. When he's gone I read the message. This time there's no envelope. It's the same piece of paper with the sentence: 'He lay awake at night, desiring her, and he had her.' Underneath he's written, 'Tomorrow I'll come and get you!'

Tomorrow — that's today. My calm evaporates.

Marianne and Gisela are in the shop. They seem to be getting to know each other, they talk about their children and Hartmut's twenty years without his family, which nobody can ever give back to him. I leave them be. There are some things which are so difficult to say, every word is a struggle; I'd only be disturbing them.

I can see Hartmut outside. He's wearing

one of Siegfried's blue boiler suits and heading for the sawmill. The children are skipping along behind him. What an adventure this must be for them.

Frieda is in the kitchen with Volker. She's summoned him from town because Hartmut wanted to see his other brother too. But the feeling is not mutual. Volker has hardly been able to look Hartmut in the eye, and for years he's been giving Siegfried a wide berth. He doesn't seem to notice that I'm there. His dull expression only seems to come to life when drink is put on the table. I can definitely see the similarities between Volker and Alfred. Volker's so different from his two brothers. There's something shifty about him, something that makes me distrust him. Acrid alcoholic fumes are polluting the entire kitchen. All that's missing is Alfred. From day one I sensed that he didn't like me, I seem to disturb him somehow. Maybe he had become used to the fixed set of people in the family. And then I came along.

★ ★ ★

If Henner really does come for me I'd like to give him a cake, so I stay in the kitchen and bake my first cake without any help. Volker and Frieda move to the parlour. Six eggs, three hundred and sixty grams of sugar, the same amount of butter and flour. No baking powder. The grated zest of one lemon, the juice of four lemons, some vanilla, a pinch of salt. Bake for sixty minutes: forty minutes at 180 degrees, twenty at 200 degrees, checking that it doesn't brown too quickly on top — this is what Frieda's always told me.

I feel very grown up here in the kitchen. The windows that give onto the yard are open, Alfred glances inside, snuffles, nods and smiles inscrutably. The others are scattered all over the farm. Then everything happens as if by magic. The cake comes out of the oven, golden-brown and smelling fantastic, and I can hear his voice in the shop and the women laughing. I bet he's flirting with them. I'm instantly envious of Gisela. She's wearing a dress today too, and her blonde hair falls in fragrant waves across her white shoulders. She smells fantastic. We couldn't work out what it was. Some mixture of rose and sandalwood, but we're too embarrassed to ask. She must think we're peasants, Marianne and me.

I can't make out what he's saying, but now Marianne is calling my name. 'Come over here, Maria!' she says. 'Henner's got his horses with him.' I've already cut the cake and wrapped it in sandwich paper. I put the package in my bag, as well as the note and a pencil.

When I enter the shop I'm reassured, for the moment at least. He may be joking with the women, but he only has eyes for me. Softly, almost casually, he says, 'There you are, Maria. I've brought the mare along; you wanted to go riding today, didn't you?'

'Yes,' I say. 'I'm coming.'

Then he helps me up into Jella's saddle; on the stallion there is just a horse blanket. 'Bring her back safe and sound, Henner!' Marianne calls out behind us. He gives a short nod, and I feel horribly deceitful.

We trot once along the woodland path by the railway tracks and then go straight back to his farmhouse. He takes the horses to the stables and shuts the main gate. I can't be sure, but I think I saw Alfred at the end of the path.

In the kitchen he makes coffee and I unwrap the cake. It's still warm and smells so lemony. Henner takes a piece and has a bite. 'Did Frieda bake this?' he asks.

I shake my head. 'No, I did.'

He grins, no doubt astonished by my efforts. 'It tastes wonderful, Maria,' he says. 'It's a long time since anybody baked me a cake.' Then his face darkens and he gives me a peculiar look. I stand up and go close to him. He pulls me onto his knees.

Then he lays me down on the kitchen table and takes me. The dogs are lying by the door, their beefy heads resting on their paws, quietly watching us.

Afterwards we drink cold coffee and smoke. There's a volume of poetry on the table. My head was on it when Henner stood behind me and lifted my skirt. One stanza is underlined, beside it are some illegible words. A woman's handwriting, I reckon; Henner didn't write that. I like the verse, even though it makes me feel melancholic:

We are the wanderers without goal,
The clouds blown away by the wind,
The flowers trembling in the chill of death,
Waiting to be mown down.

'My mother's,' he says. 'All the books were hers.' He stares at me. 'She wasn't cut out for farm work either. Like you.' And then he talks to me for ages about his mother; all I'd heard about her was that she was a drinker, and a bit of an oddball.

Henner's mother — Helene Henner, née Mannsfeld, then Bechert in her first marriage — was thirty-five by the time she had him. She was born in 1915 into a middle-class family in Berlin. She was an only child. Her father died in the war, in a military hospital following the amputation of both his arms. Things got more and more difficult for the family. The mother's money lasted a few years more, but by the beginning of the 1930s it was all gone. She never married again, Helene's mother.

Helene went to a good school, she was well educated and had fine manners, just no money. She was eighteen when she met the lawyer Ernst Bechert, and she married him immediately, despite her lack of funds. Ernst built up his career and became a member of the Nazi Party. They had no children. In 1940 he was conscripted and returned in February 1945 with a serious head injury and only one eye. But when the Russians came he hanged himself in the kitchen of their flat. Helene couldn't get away in time. The streets were already teeming with Russian soldiers, and it was hard to disguise her beauty even beneath a dirty headscarf. They got her in the cellar. She didn't know how many there were, but it must have been dozens. One injured her so badly that the others, who'd been waiting their turn, no longer wanted this half-dead woman. She must have bled like a slaughtered animal, and it went on like that for weeks. She confessed all this to her second husband on his deathbed, and it was only then that he understood everything.

In the summer of 1945 she dragged her battered body out of the city. No-one knows for sure how she made it to Thuringia and our village. She was given work and a little room at the Henners' farm, and a year later she married Franz, the youngest son, who had survived the war in spite of a few frostbitten toes and large amounts of shrapnel. He was twenty-nine, she thirty-one. The two other brothers at the farm had died in the war.

Henner was born in 1950. Nobody had imagined they would ever have a child. During her pregnancy, Helene acquired a great number of books and, to the consternation of the Henner family, spent her days reading. Later she disappeared completely into her books and her schnapps, and never surfaced again.

★ ★ ★

Henner lays his head in my lap with a sigh, and I cover it with my dress. Then he starts to cry. Yes, he cries, and his tears wet my bare legs, which are still trembling. It was the only time I ever saw him like this, and never again. Love made him soft.

8

Back home at the Brendels' farm, Marianne is there to meet me. 'That was a long ride,' she says. As I walk past her she suddenly leans into me and takes a sniff. I'll never forget how her nose practically brushes my neck. When she looks up at me I hold my breath, regretting not having washed off Henner's scent. Suddenly she smiles and says, 'You smell like a stable! Go and have a quick shower before supper.' I nod silently. This time I've got away with it.

★ ★ ★

Hartmut's definitely taken some colour. He got up early with Siegfried and helped him with the day's work. His cheeks are red and he swallows down his food greedily. Gisela keeps glancing over at him, but doesn't say anything. The children are winding Lukas up and talking incessantly. We're not used to such chitter-chatter at the table. Alfred's eyes scan the room grumpily, then his gaze rests on me. I stare into my wine glass, sweating.

Out of the blue, Hartmut asks whether we

are going to take a look at our Stasi files when the time comes, if they haven't all been destroyed by then. Siegfried laughs and says he doesn't need to; he already knows what's in his and who supplied the information. Then he turns to me and says, 'The only one around this table who has an unblemished record — if she has one at all — is Maria.' That comment made me want to fling my supper in his face. I mean, I was at the first demonstration in P., chanting 'We are the people!' along with the rest of them. O.K., I admit we weren't there just because of the demonstration; our plan was to go to the ice-cream parlour afterwards, my friend Katja and I. But Siegfried doesn't stop his teasing. 'Maria,' he says with a grave expression, his arms crossed, 'went to Pioneer Camp. Top marks for your file, that. It's where they groomed our future elite, isn't that right, Maria?' I'm close to tears. What does he know about Pioneer Camp? Gisela looks nonplussed, so I have to explain, keeping an eye on Siegfried the whole time. He does actually shut up, and by the end he's even turned a little pale.

I was twelve, top of the class, and deputy chair of the friendship council at Erich Weinert Secondary School in R. One day Mum and I were called in to see the headmistress. She told us that I had been chosen from our district to go to the Wilhelm Pieck Pioneer Camp. For six weeks. In school time. It was an honour you didn't turn down. And so, in February 1986, I went by train to Berlin with lots of other children from various districts and a group of Pioneer leaders. From there we were bused to the camp on the shore of Lake Werbellin. The first day was a disaster. I didn't have a Pioneer's cap, I used a Scout's knot to tie the red neckerchief rather than a Pioneer one, and I didn't have a badge on the arm of my white blouse. I'd never had a blouse with the badge. My mother always let me wear cardigans on top and nobody had minded. At the first major flag parade I had to stand at one end of the back row, then in the middle of the square formation, where I was reprimanded for showing insufficient respect for the Pioneer organisation, and by extension the German Democratic Republic. Later I was called in to the office of the duty Pioneer leader. A message was sent to my mother via the council offices in our village. That same day she sent a package with the items I was missing. And three days later I looked like all the other girls: dark-blue skirt, white Pioneer blouse, neckerchief tied with the proper knot, and a blue cap on my head.

There was no end to the rules and regulations: how you were supposed to arrange your clothes over the chair every evening when you undressed, the neckerchief always on top; how to make your bed with military precision; when you had to get up for early-morning exercises, barked at by loudspeakers, which were in every block and throughout the camp grounds. A marching song accompanied our exercises; I can only remember the chorus:

Pioneers to the fore, onwards with a
  spring!
Pioneers to the core, wave the banner
  as we sing!
We march towards the morning sun,
  proud Pioneers all and one!

This was followed by a long day in the classroom, including extra Russian tuition and citizenship lessons. We ate our meals in a large hall where cockroaches scuttled under the tables. I'd never seen a cockroach before and thought they were really disgusting. We had flag parade three times a day, and each one began with the announcement 'Thälmann Pioneers, be prepared!' and ended with the answer 'Always prepared!' In the evenings we watched the news bulletin and sometimes Karl-Eduard von Schnitzler's political propaganda programme.

On one of them they featured a West German fruit and vegetable stall with beautiful shiny produce. But then the reporter turned over a few pieces of fruit and pointed to brown spots and mould. We shuddered. 'As you can see, all that glisters is not gold,' the Pioneer leader said triumphantly. In the next scene we saw a homeless man holding out a dirty hand, begging. We were shocked.

We all wrote diaries; they told us to, and it wasn't long before we discovered why. One morning a supervisor came and collected all the diaries. The following day our entries were displayed for all to see in the foyers of the dormitory blocks. Our thoughts became public property. Here nothing belonged to any one individual, or, to put it another way, everything belonged to everybody.

Objects or toys which clearly came from foreign, imperialist countries were confiscated. Amongst my belongings were a pencil case with a small British flag and a nightie printed with an American cartoon character. I'd been sent the occasional parcel of second-hand clothes from one of Mum's distant relatives in the West.

My dormitory comrades had no offensive items in their possession.

The letters I sent home were returned to me opened, and then I was summoned to the

Pioneer leaders' office. There were three people sitting there, and one of them read out my letters. After the first I already had trouble concentrating, and I tried to work out whether the person walking along the path outside was Silke, the only friend I'd made up till then. It was hard to tell, she was wearing the same as the rest of us. At that point they ordered me to listen, but I knew the words off by heart — they were always the same: 'Dear Mama, the camp is like a prison. Please come and take me home. I can't stay here. I'm so unhappy and I cry all the time, especially at night. Love, Maria.' They told me that if I wrote anything like that again there'd be serious trouble for me and my parents, more serious than I could possibly imagine.

After that I wasn't frightened any more. It couldn't get any worse, I thought. And in fact it didn't. My mother never got the letters, and nobody came to take me home. But halfway through the six weeks I no longer wanted to leave. There had been a torchlight procession. All of us, hundreds of children, had marched through a sea of fire that surged left and right, singing 'The Little Trumpeter' and 'Peat Bog Soldiers'. The torches showed us the way across the camp to a large parade square, where the procession stopped. To finish we sang the last verse of 'Peat Bog Soldiers'.

That was my turning point, something snapped inside me, my resistance dissolved. I felt at one with the others, strong and invincible. It was an uplifting moment, indescribable, and at the same time one of the most unsettling aspects of my entire stay.

When Gisela asks to hear the song again and I launch into 'Peat Bog Soldiers' — with a certain frisson of excitement — it's not long before Siegfried, Hartmut, Marianne, Alfred and Frieda join in, in that very order.

Far and wide as the eye can wander,
Heath and bog are everywhere.
Not a bird sings out to cheer us,
Oaks are standing gaunt and bare.
We are the peat bog soldiers.
We're marching with our spades to the
    bog.

Marianne hums the tune in her clear voice, because she doesn't know the words, and when we get to the final verse — 'But for us there is no complaining, / Winter will in time be past. / One day we shall cry rejoicing, 'Homeland dear you're mine at last!'' — there's no stopping Siegfried. He belts out the words so loudly that the rest of us fall silent, and Gisela grips onto her chair with both hands. None of us says a word and I feel a bit embarrassed for Siegfried. We're all thinking our own thoughts, and when the silence goes on for too long I embark on the conclusion to my story. When, after six weeks, I came home and sang Russian war songs at the dinner table, my mother asked me in tears, 'What on earth have they done to you?' I cried and missed my friends. It took me a while to get used to being at home again, and my yearning for camp life eventually turned into a rejection of everything collective.

★ ★ ★

Siegfried had no idea that it had been like that. Now he looks at me rather sympathetically. Gisela finds it all 'barbaric', like under the Nazis; Hartmut agrees with her, even though he's been singing along heartily too. 'Bastards!' he says repeatedly. 'Miserable bastards! They broke children in those camps.' Then Frieda brings in the pudding. Tiramisu. We've never had it before. Even the name sounds exciting. Gisela made it; she brought the ingredients with her. I wonder whether Hartmut is right, whether they really broke me, but on balance I think he's exaggerating.

None of us noticed Johannes taking photographs of us while we were singing. Tonight, when he develops them, I'll be able to see how Alfred was looking at me. We go to bed late, very late, and Johannes holds me gently in his arms.

In the other room is my bag and another note from Henner. I'm saving it for tomorrow.

9

I've been neglecting *The Brothers Karamazov*. I left it at the point where something dreadful happened. Fyodor Karamazov is dead. Murdered, and all the evidence suggests his son, Dmitry, is the culprit. But in the midst of the greatest adversity, and when he no longer cares about anything, Grushenka shows him her love. There are times when love saves everything.

Before I start the next chapter, I take out Henner's note and read it. 'Come and stay with me, just for a day . . . ' Every time I read his words it's as if the ground has fallen away beneath me, and every time I feel like running away and leaving it all behind, even Johannes. But I don't. I harbour the same sense of foreboding Zossima had when he bowed down before Dmitry. I have no idea what it might be, Henner's future suffering, but I fear it may have something to do with me.

Downstairs they're sitting all together at the breakfast table. The children have been absorbed by the farm. They romp about in the animal sheds and in the meadows, and only appear at mealtimes. I don't feel like eating. I'm completely full; Henner doesn't leave room for much else. Johannes is telling them how he met me: at that first demonstration in P. Thousands of people were there; the march was so long we couldn't see where it began or ended. Carried by the throng, we surged past the big department store and then headed for the marketplace. 'We are the people! We are the people!' the masses shouted, and it felt the same as it had when I was in Pioneer Camp, except that there the feeling had been even stronger, perhaps because of the torches and songs.

Katja and I were exhausted from all the chanting, and were about to slip away to the ice-cream parlour when suddenly we noticed a water cannon just a few metres away. People started screaming, others kept chanting 'We are the people!', and somehow I lost Katja and she lost me. A woman was pushing a pram alongside me. Police with machine guns were everywhere. Aiming at us. Then came the jet of water. The woman with the baby stumbled, the pram shot off sideways and rolled into the crowd. A man stopped it and took out the child. The baby was screaming its head off, the woman was on the ground, howling and howling, and when the man pulled her up, the baby almost slipped from his grasp. I put my hands in front of my face and didn't move. Everyone was running all over the place, but nobody ran away. They're going to shoot, I thought. They're just going to take aim and whoever's at the front is going to get it. I was at the front. Katja hadn't reappeared. But now Johannes was beside me — we'd known each other since kindergarten — and he wrenched me away, through the crowd, then into a side street. We ran and ran, without knowing where we were going, and behind us there was a huge commotion. Something had happened, but we couldn't see anything any more. He dragged me into a doorway, pushed the door open and shoved me inside. And there he kissed me for the first time. It was October 1989. It felt as if we'd escaped with our lives, even though in hindsight it turned out that nothing serious had happened.

★　★　★

Gisela is staring in astonishment, and also in slight disbelief, as if Johannes were recounting a fairy tale. She must think he's been exaggerating. But she's wrong. Johannes tends to play things down; he hasn't even really captured the drama of the story. But it's obviously enough for Gisela. Seeing how shocked she is by this makes me wonder whether Hartmut actually told her the truth about prison. Does she know that they left him for three days with a high temperature and pneumonia before fetching a doctor? That's what he told Siegfried, who told Marianne, who told Johannes; and now I know too. But I'm not sure about Gisela. Has Hartmut kept that from her? And if so, why?

But then I think about my own secret and realise that there are things which can be said straightaway, others need time, and some cannot be told at all.

*　*　*

Of course there was more to this story. At some point we began our long journey home and found Katja at the station. When she saw us she burst into tears and threw her arms around me. We took the forty-five-minute train journey back and she walked back to the village. I went on with Johannes to the Brendels', to the barn where we spent hours kissing in the hay. Katja was given the task of telling my mother.

A few days later we were summoned to the headmistress' office, each of us in turn. I had to explain where I had been on the day of the demonstration, and ultimately what my reasons were for being there. I still don't know who betrayed us, but Katja spent less time in the office than I did.

It was a time when I often stood out from the crowd. I had decided not to take part in the state initiation ceremony and got confirmed instead, putting a stain on my otherwise spotless C.V. Siegfried was wrong when he said I had an unblemished record.

There were several reasons for my refusal to attend the initiation ceremony along with everyone else from my class. Back then I was a regular at the parsonage. One of the pastor's sons, David, came to our house quite often too. He used to climb over the fence and bring me presents. The pastor's family had frequent visitors from the West, and David was well supplied with things like chocolate, gummi bears, posters of rock stars, and sometimes records. We'd sit in my mother's bedroom and listen to banned music. I was madly in love with him. I'd have supper with his family every few days, and when we said grace before dinner — 'Come, Lord Jesus, be our guest; and bless what you have bestowed' — I uttered the words more fervently even than the pastor's children. None of them was in the Pioneers, nor in the Free German Youth; they talked about subjects that were new to me, and they were smarter than anybody else in our village. My admiration for them was boundless.

And then — this was still long before the Wall came down — the whole of Class 8 were given the initiation pledge to learn at home. We were supposed to prepare ourselves for the forthcoming ceremony; the text began with the following words:

Dear young friends!
If, as young citizens of our German Democratic Republic, you are loyal to the constitution and ready to work and fight together with us for the great and noble cause of Socialism, and honour the revolutionary legacy of the people, then answer:
Yes, this we do pledge!

David told me I couldn't say that in all seriousness, and that I ought to think about what I *would* actually say. He also claimed there were people who just disappeared because they were hostile to the state. He'd heard this from his father, and his father would never lie. And around that time, one of my mother's brothers had come to visit and told us of a friend who had been arrested two years previously for the possession and distribution of imperialist literature, including the works of some foreign philosophers. He was imprisoned in Bautzen, released a year later, and died shortly afterwards of a particularly rapid and aggressive cancer. He was twenty-nine and the father of two children. There was lots of whispering between Mum and her brother, and from what I could make out they believed it had something to do with the prison — they'd made him ill while he was inside. I couldn't get this man out of my head, and now I did find the words 'great and noble cause of Socialism' unutterable. The postwoman's son disappeared too, after he'd clambered blind drunk up a flagpole in the village, yelling 'Fucking country!' over and over. Anton was his name, and we never saw him again. David said I couldn't ignore the signs.

There were more parts to the pledge, the final one being:

If, as a true patriot, you are ready to strengthen our firm friendship with the Soviet Union, consolidate the fraternal bond between the Socialist countries, fight in the spirit of proletarian internationalism, protect peace and defend Socialism against all imperialist attacks, then answer:
Yes, this we do pledge!

I had a problem with this part of the pledge which was purely personal. I had no desire to strengthen our friendship with the Soviet

Union for the simple reason that my father had left us for a Soviet woman. He'd vanished into the heart of Soviet territory, having already spent most of the year at the gas pipeline. So I had my very own animosity towards the U.S.S.R. I absolutely loathed it, and I hated the language too, even though it came in useful; I could read the letters Mum kept finding in my father's pockets, and found out what he was up to in the Soviet Union.

In any case, my longing for the colour and diversity of the West was by now immense. I wanted to have all those things too. I didn't want to fight against them, I wanted to *own* them. But the greatest reason of all was my first love, David, for whose sake I would have done almost anything.

So my mind was made up. Mum cried a lot and said I was as stubborn as my father, if not more so. I knew the trouble in store for me, but in the end it wasn't as bad as all that. I was determined and started learning by heart catechisms, verses from the Bible and the Nicene Creed — for God, as David's father liked to say, was greater than Socialism.

★   ★   ★

I didn't go into all that detail, however. The little I had told Gisela was more than enough

95

for her already. She seems not to want to know the truth about a world she has only ever regarded with pity and slight contempt from the other side of the Wall. She shies away from conversations like this and keeps her distance from us. I saw how she took Hartmut's hand and placed it anxiously in hers, as if she were worried he might slip away from her, dive into the past and stay there.

The conversation swings round to Volker. Nobody knows for sure why he started drinking. It wasn't as if everybody else in the agricultural collective drank. And apart from the frequent arguments he had with his father, his life wasn't too bad. I wouldn't be at all surprised if he were Alfred's son. Maybe he's sensed it, because certainly nobody's told him. A lie consumes people from the inside, Grandma Traudel always says. You can keep the lid on it for ages, but at some point it boils over — I've often heard her say that. I'm sure Volker's drinking has something to do with this. When he was younger he even had a girlfriend. For a while they lived together at the farm, up in the attic rooms where Johannes and I are now staying. But Siegfried and Volker argued, and because Siegfried was the more capable of the two, Volker eventually had to go. He held it against everybody, especially Alfred, who on that occasion backed

Siegfried even though he generally took Volker's side. But Volker was unreliable. When he drank, he forgot about the animals, and no-one would tolerate that.

Frieda goes into the sitting room. She doesn't like talking about Volker, but she loves him nonetheless; after all, he is her eldest son. Alfred trudges after her in silence. And now Siegfried says something which takes everyone by surprise. He says, 'If I checked my Stasi file to see who had informed on me, whose name do you think I'd find there?' He grins impishly and looks around. Marianne claps her hand over her mouth and Hartmut shakes his head. Gisela goes from one face to another and Johannes says, 'I can imagine, Dad.'

And because Volker knows that Siegfried knows, he doesn't like coming to the farm any more.

Then we leave them at the table. Johannes takes my hand, leading me out into the hallway and up the stairs. His mind is on other things; he has a plan. He wants to go to Leipzig to look around the art college. It's vacation time at the moment, but someone will be there, he says. He hasn't asked whether I want to go with him. This is his road, and mine — this much I know — is currently heading in a different direction. It's too early to say where. I'm lurching from one emotional state to another, living from one day to the next, always in the present, always in the now, and the now is Henner. Johannes and the future are unknowns.

10

Some days have passed. Dismal days, sad days, during which I've heard nothing from Henner nor seen him. He hasn't even come to the shop. Marianne says he must be on a bender, or with some woman. This makes me frantic. But it's my turn to answer him. 'Come and stay with me, just for a day . . . ' His message was quite clear; it's up to me.

★ ★ ★

Gisela and Hartmut have returned to Bavaria, taking Frieda with them. It's her first ever trip abroad — we are still the G.D.R., after all. She was so excited that Marianne had to pack her case for her; Frieda had no idea what to bring. Normally she wears her apron dress day in, day out. Hartmut has promised to visit more often; he wants to be around to help Siegfried when the family gets the land back from the collective. And he's more interested in those files than the rest of us put together.

★ ★ ★

I don't know what to do. I've been over to Henner's farm a few times, but it's all locked up. Johannes went off to Leipzig yesterday and won't be back for three days. I decide to go to the tavern, to ask whether the landlord needs any waitressing help for the rest of the summer. He's opened a beer garden, and even tourists are beginning to come to this part of the world now. I make myself look nice: I put on a clean, pale-coloured dress, a little lipstick and my shoes with the low heels. Then I wander along the dusty lane to the tavern. It is early afternoon, hot and without a breath of wind. There's a faint buzzing in the air.

When I enter the tavern I see Henner at the regulars' table. He's paralytic, and railing against the 'criminal state that's fucked up my life. Even my wife buggered off — she was with the Stasi, the old slut.' Straightaway my knees start trembling. He looks terrible: dirty, brutal — not at all how I'd like to see him. I steel myself and go over to the bar, then ask the landlord for a quiet word, hoping that Henner won't notice me. His right hand, in a sticky pool of beer, is gripping the table for support, his left hand rests limply on his stained trouser leg. Don't turn around, Henner, I say to myself, but that's exactly what he does. He looks up at me, grins with a demented glint in his eye, and gives a brief chuckle. 'Maria! The little doll!' he bellows. 'It's all so easy for her, she's moving away from here and never coming back. Never! What does she see in Johannes, that boy?' And then he laughs so loudly that even the other drinkers look slightly embarrassed. My whole body is shaking, and the landlord says, 'Fantastic, you can start next week. I really need the help this summer as Gabi's expecting another child and she can't do much at the moment.'

Then I leave the room and just head off. I don't know where I'm going, but instinctively I take the path to the woods. And when I've been walking for a long time, really quite far, I hear a panting behind me. Before I can work out what's happening he's overtaken me. He pulls me to the ground and the two of us collapse in a heap. Henner is lying on top of me and holds me tight. Until I stop struggling. Then he kneels over me and, with a sobriety to match his drunkenness in the tavern, says, 'Now you're coming with me!' I wipe the woodland earth from my dress and race back to the farm. After telling Marianne that I'm going to see my mother and don't know when I'll be back, I fetch what I need from the spiders' nest, stash a few vegetables and a piece of meat from the shop in my bag, and leave. I'm sure I would have gone

101

even if Johannes had been here. I wouldn't have thought twice about it.

★ ★ ★

By the time I arrive he's washed and put on fresh clothes. I'm astonished by how quickly he's sobered up. I don't want to talk yet; I punish him with my silence. Then I start chopping vegetables. I sweat the onions and garlic in butter, add the finely diced potatoes and the rest of the vegetables, some spices which I find in his kitchen, and cook for a quarter of an hour, stirring in a little cream and some flour. Then the meat: two thick sirloins, juicy and tender. 'Set the table, Henner,' I say. 'It'll be ready soon.' All of a sudden he looks quite young. A sneer creeps across his face. But he sets the table without answering back.

He watches me throughout the meal, as if to make sure that I don't disappear again. I like that, though I know I'm being vain and arrogant. I want him to look at me, desire me, me alone and no other. Me alone.

When we get up from the table and go to the other room I say something to him, something which I already know I will never say again. 'Do what you want with me,' I whisper into his ear. And he does.

* * *

The next morning I'm woken by the dogs barking. Someone must be at the door, or maybe it's just an animal. Needing to pee I try to get up. I lift my legs from the bed and lower them onto the cool floor, but they collapse beneath me. Henner hastens over and carries me to the bathroom and back again. It reminds me of cats who drag their little ones around between their teeth. Today Henner is my mother cat. I did cry a little last night, and at one point I asked him to stop. He replied quietly, but with an odd tone to his voice, that I should have thought about that earlier; now it was too late.

* * *

The dogs are quiet again, and Henner is washing me with a warm sponge. He strokes the hair from my face and wants to make me pure again. Then he makes tea and goes into the village to fetch some rolls. He stays with me all day, feeding and cleaning me. I'm not at all well. My head is hot and my mind scrambled, yet I feel happy. Just so long as he doesn't leave my bedside; that makes me anxious. At dusk he puts a small lamp on the floor by the bed and starts reading a poem to me: 'With your cool, kind hands / Close all wounds / So that they bleed inwardly / Sweet mother of pain, you!' I close my eyes and slide back into my fever. 'In silence the darkness extinguished me / I became a dead shadow in the day / Then I stepped from the hearth of joy / Out into the night. / . . . / You are in deep midnight / An unbegotten in a sweet womb / And never being, unformed! / You are in deep midnight.' Later I feel his cool hands on my feverish body, but I no longer know whether I'm awake or dreaming.

Grushenka, Grushenka, will you really stay with Dmitry?

That night he lies next to me and tosses and turns, getting no sleep. The fever alters my perception. It seems as if several metres are separating Henner and me, though I can touch him. Even my own arms and legs seem to be moving away from me. I abandon myself to this sensation, and lying on my tummy, my head on my arms, I doze off. Later I feel him inside me again. He takes me as he pleases — until he's finally able to get to sleep.

One day turns into two, and I'm still here on the third day. Henner says I talked a lot in my delirium, but none of it made any sense.

I still feel so weak, and Johannes is coming

back today. If he sees I'm not at the farm he'll drive over to Mum's to fetch me. Then it will all come out.

There are lots of empty cups beside the bed. Henner made herbal teas and spooned them into my mouth, at least that's what he says. I can't remember anything.

I'm feeling uneasy; I must get back to the farm before Johannes. I need to go. Now. Henner has washed my clothes and brings them to me in bed. He looks at me for a long time. His eyes are asking what I remember of these nights, whether he went too far. I leave him with his unspoken question; I don't know the answer myself.

Daylight enters the dark room. After struggling to get dressed I step out of the house as if out of time. Everything inside is old. The walls, the bed, and somehow Henner too. He walks me to the gate and says, 'I'm here, Maria, you know that.' This time he doesn't give me a note as I leave.

★ ★ ★

Alfred is standing and watching at the Brendels' front door. He gives me a Frieda-like greeting, says, 'Oh, so she's back. Did she have a nice time at her mother's?' A mischievous grin forms on his thin lips, and he narrows his

eyes. But before I can answer him the Wartburg comes to a stop behind me and Johannes
gets out. My heart is pounding and I can feel
a throbbing in my head. Lying is the worst
sin, Grandma Traudel used to say when Lorenz
was having one of his wild spells. I think she's
right.

11

Johannes is so excited about the last few days, thank God, that he doesn't notice how quiet I am. This time he's the one talking nineteen to the dozen, about the city, which still looks horribly grey, about the people he met at the art college and the specialist photography course they run there. One of the students told him that the photos he brought with him were really good. He's got an eye for light and composition — those were the exact words. 'Light and composition,' Johannes repeats reverently.

Then he wants to take my dress off and I go rigid. Since I've got my period I don't have to lie. It started yesterday at Henner's, and I didn't have anything on me. He just put some thick towels on the sheets, changing them often. He wasn't at all fazed. I don't think Johannes could have done that.

We get around to talking about the city, and about the portfolio that Johannes needs to put together if he applies. He wants to make a series about the village: its inhabitants and their houses, both inside and out. It can't be too documentary, as he puts it, it has to be art, and art looks different. I couldn't say how an artistic photograph differs from a documentary one, but Johannes is in the process of explaining it to me. And yet his words don't reach me.

Later I tell him about my summer job at the tavern. He thinks it's a good idea, because he's going to be spending most of the coming weeks taking photos and working in the darkroom. He goes in there now, and I breathe a sigh of relief.

I'm not the same girl I once was. But who am I?

★　★　★

The heat up in our attic rooms forces me outside; I take *The Brothers Karamazov* with me.

Lukas is down in the shop today, helping his mother. Marianne is in a shockingly bad mood. Since Frieda went off to Bavaria she's had twice as much work to do. Frieda cooks for the entire family, and now Marianne has to do it herself, even though she's not that great in the kitchen. Frieda should be back in a week. She rang once; she called the co-op and Marianne went scooting over there. Apparently Frieda didn't sound happy; in fact she just grumbled the whole time.

Marianne brings up the subject of the meat that I took, which Henner found so delicious. She says sternly, 'It's sweet of you to bring your mother something, but you can't just take it without asking.' She's absolutely right, and I swear blind that next time I'll ask her permission.

★　★　★

Out in the meadow the grass has grown tall again. It is August, and another hay harvest is imminent. I lie on the riverbank with *The Brothers Karamazov*, and as I start reading I realise that it all sounds familiar, even though I can't have read it before. This continues for dozens of pages. I'm quite sure I hadn't got this far — I'd used a bookmark — and yet I know what is about to happen.

Dmitry isn't the murderer. It was the servant Smerdyakov, probably an illegal child of the old — and now dead — Fyodor Karamazov. He claims that the middle brother, Ivan, gave him the idea of committing the murder. But this doesn't exonerate Dmitry in the slightest, as there's no statement, and the day before the trial begins, Smerdyakov hangs himself. People say of Grushenka that she was the undoing of both father and son. The city women are especially malicious about her.

The swallows are flying low above me — rain is on its way. I can see Siegfried by the weir in the distance. He's getting more cheerful by the day, on account of the grand plans he's been hatching. His new buzzwords are 'biodynamic agriculture', which Hartmut talked about at length. In Bavaria, he said, there were so-called 'Demeter' farms, cultivating in much the same way as Siegfried on his farm, but getting a decent sum of money for their products. There was a specific philosophy behind it, and the name Rudolf Steiner cropped up. It was all about 'living interactions' and 'cosmic rhythms in crop farming'. At that point Marianne almost fell over laughing, and kept repeating the words 'cosmic rhythms' as she danced mysteriously about the kitchen. She can be rather silly sometimes, even though she's not young any more — well, she's younger than Henner, but that's different. But Hartmut was undeterred, and quoting this Steiner, he said, 'A farm is true to its essential nature, in the best sense of the word, if it is conceived as a kind of individual entity in itself.' Siegfried grasped the meaning of this at once, while Marianne was still chortling with laughter, and Frieda and Alfred just shook their heads. 'It's a philosophy, Mother,' Hartmut tried to explain, but it was no good. Then he talked about the 'animal as a creature with a soul' and the importance of the ruminant for the quality of the soil. The animal must be able, Hartmut said, 'to relate to its environment via its senses'. 'This means,' he concluded solemnly, because we were all looking at him with puzzled expressions, 'that the cow must go to the pasture!' Marianne couldn't control herself any longer.

When Siegfried had had enough of his wife's cackling and his mother's head-shaking, he went out into the meadows with Hartmut and Gisela. Taking exception to this Marianne said to Frieda, 'They obviously think we're a little thick here in the East, them and their animals with souls.' But then she took out an encyclopedia and looked up 'Demeter'. She found the picture of the goddess rather beautiful and asked us whether we agreed that she looked a little like Demeter. In truth you couldn't deny a certain similarity.

★ ★ ★

I'd love to know what Siegfried is thinking, the way he's standing there, his legs planted firmly on the ground and his eyes roaming the countryside.

That evening I join the family again at the

table. Alfred has already gone to bed. Ever since Frieda left he has seemed somehow unwell. There is a lot of talk today, much more than usual. Siegfried is planning a visit to one of those farms, to see what makes them so special. 'It's not magic, it's farming,' he says, and now Marianne is nodding enthusiastically. Johannes starts talking about his application to art college and his father raises no objections, which surprises us all. His only suggestion is that Johannes should take his time, have a thorough look at the college and, if it's not right for him, he can come back home. There's going to be plenty of work on the farm in the future. Later we all drink wine, and then an argument flares up which proves uncomfortable for everyone.

Marianne seldom drinks, but when she does she has little self-control and she'll put away a whole bottle of wine by herself. Our tongues are loosened, there's much laughter, but then the conversation turns to Henner. Siegfried says Henner's best years are behind him; there's not much left in the tank. The G.D.R. took it all out of him. Marianne comes to Henner's defence, says he's still quite dashing, and just lately he's become much more affable. Something must have happened, she says, for him to be in such good form, and if he could just leave off the booze, surely he'd be able to whip the farm into shape again. 'You like old Henner, don't you?' Siegfried says, and then Marianne says something which must have been the wine talking, but maybe there's some truth to it, deep down: 'I wouldn't kick him out of bed if I didn't have you, Siggi.' Those are her exact words. This is all way too much for Siegfried, and for Johannes too, who gives his mother a filthy look. She notices immediately and shuts up, which is all well and good, but now it's out of the bag and the evening is ruined. Another subject comes up for discussion. This one must have been brewing for a while, and Siegfried can't keep it bottled up any longer. It's about the housekeeping. Money has started disappearing from the pot, something that never used to happen. Meanwhile, small tubes of fancy face creams and bottles of perfume have appeared in the bathroom, and lying about in the sitting room are magazines with flawless-looking women on the covers. The West has given rise to these material desires, and a woman like Marianne finds it hard to resist them. But all this leaves Siegfried cold. He couldn't care less whether or not his wife's skin feels softer, or whether she smells of hay or lilac. I imagine he might prefer hay. We don't know whether it was the saucy comment about Henner or the money wasted which got Siegfried so irate, but he gets up, takes an empty wine bottle and smashes it against the edge of the table. Then he screams, 'You're not going to make a fool of me, Marianne — others have already tried and regretted it!' He storms out of the room and into the yard, still screaming: 'You just can't trust women! It'll always be the same! Bloody women!' He doesn't come back until late. Johannes says he's seen his father like that only once before. It was at the village party two years ago when Marianne danced rather too intimately with the landlord's brother, whom everybody knew was with the Stasi. Both of them were drunk, and alcohol doesn't bring out the best in Siegfried, even though he's generally a reasonable man.

That time he dragged her home, and when they were up in their room he hit her. Lukas was in bed next door and heard everything.

This scene has left me feeling miserable. I wish I were with Henner, I wish I were free. I'd live with him for as long as it worked. And when it stopped working I'd stay anyway.

12

The following morning Siegfried is in the animal sheds by five o'clock as usual. His determination, his strength, his sense of duty — these are the reasons Marianne has always admired him, and why she loves him still. Yesterday evening's outburst was an aberration in almost twenty years of marriage; by and large they have been good years. By midday the dark clouds have already blown over, only to gather again when Henner appears in the shop.

He buys meat, salami, potatoes, leeks, tomatoes and a punnet of raspberries. He's not here because of me, but he looks pleased when I come to serve him instead of Marianne. She hardly dares glance at him, even though he cannot know about last night's argument. She's relieved when Siegfried calls for her help in one of the meadows. Maybe he just wanted to get her away. I've come to realise that in matters of the heart, older folk are just as foolish as younger ones. I'm left on my own with Henner. Johannes and Lukas have gone to town to get something for their father. There's only

Alfred, and he's easy to forget, given the way he sneaks around the place so inconspicuously.

I pack his shopping into a paper bag and put it on the counter. 'Come here, Maria,' he says. 'I want to feel you.' He gives the door a kick and it swings to, but doesn't shut completely. All of a sudden I am struck by an urge to sink to the ground at his feet. Where this comes from I have no idea. But he pushes aside his shopping and hoists me up onto the counter. His hands roam at will and I say, 'Are you insane? What if Marianne comes in?'

This does not seem to bother him, and he asks, 'When are you coming over again?' Then he pauses and whispers, 'I've got used to having you there.' His smile is genuine, and it pains me. He strokes my hair, arms, neck, lips; he's soft, and a little sad as well. My surrender during those feverish nights was like a promise, and now he's coming and demanding it be fulfilled.

There is a movement at the door. It might have been the cat, or some other creature slinking about.

Henner rolls up my dress. 'I hurt you,' he says without looking me in the eye. 'But I'm not sorry for it.' His hands are resting on my legs. 'Say something, Maria, say something!'

But I don't know what to say. My hesitation is not for the reason he thinks. I can't find the right words; all I feel is a vague fear which rears up from some dark corner and vanishes again in a flash. Not for me, no. For him. That's all I know.

It's Alfred at the door, I'm sure of it. I think he's known for ages. He has eyes in the back of his head, because no-one takes him seriously. It makes him almost invisible.

'I don't know when I can come. Here they're beginning to wonder why I keep on going home to my mother. And what happens if they bump into Mum in town and ask about me? What then?'

'I don't know, Maria,' he says with a shrug, and I'm so disappointed by his answer that I push his hands away and swing over to the other side of the counter. He must have seen his failure in my eyes, for he comes round, grabs me by the wrists and says with the certainty I had wanted to hear, 'You're coming anyway!'

Then we hear the car out in the yard. 'Hi, Henner,' Johannes says as he enters. He comes behind the counter and gives me a kiss, but Henner has already gone. It's all so sordid and yet I'm still going along with it.

Johannes asks when lunch will be ready, but there's nothing happening in the kitchen.

117

We all realise how much we're missing Frieda. I start preparing lunch; I've learned a lot over the past few weeks. Later, Siegfried praises my cooking — he said he was amazed by how good it was. Strange that I'm trying to distance myself from the family just as my place within it is becoming more secure. No-one here has any sense of the finer things in life. 'Maria,' Siegfried says, 'who would have thought?'

★ ★ ★

I owe my name to my mother's nostalgia. As the daughter of a communist she rarely went to church, but once she saw a nativity play and the girl playing Mary made such an impression on her that she used to wish she were called Maria too. She's a northerner, my mother; she never felt at home here in Thuringia. She loathes the rolling landscape that I love so much. When she was pregnant with me my father packed her things and simply took her with him. She cried the whole way, not stopping until they reached the village where I was born. When she went into labour she really ought to have gone to hospital, but because my father and grand-parents were not there, and she couldn't make it to the nearest telephone in the co-op,

I entered this world on my grandparents' kitchen floor. Looking back, my mother wasn't at all unhappy about this. Other women had told her that in hospital they took the babies away at birth, and they only saw them every four hours for feeding. But she was able to keep me. She didn't put me down for days, apart from the odd spell in my crib, and then only so that she could sit beside me and stare. At least this is what my grandmother told me; she wouldn't stop moaning about it at the time, but now she no longer mentions it.

We would go up north whenever we could, and there were always tears when we said our goodbyes. It was on one of those holidays to my mother's parents that I saw the West for the first time. We took a trip to the small town of D. The border strip, with its tall, barbed-wire fence, ran alongside one of the streets. One of my mother's relatives lived on the third floor of an apartment block in that street. You could see the West from her windows. Beyond the River Elbe and across the meadows stood a solitary house, which I'd never be able to visit. I can quite clearly remember what I thought and felt that day. I must have been around seven, and I couldn't take my eyes off this house. How on earth could people live only a few hundred metres away, and yet we'd never get to meet them? I mean, we could almost see them! And they us. We could have waved to each other, or signalled with lights, like I used to back home with our neighbour's son. I got stomach cramps and didn't want to eat any of the cake, even though it had strawberries on top.

When we left my uncle's flat and came out onto the street, I ran over to the fence and stuck my nose through the wire. My mother called me back — in the end she had to drag me away — the dogs behind the fence were yelping, and a soldier raised his rifle and screamed, 'Get away from the fence!'

You never forget something like that.

It's been almost a year since we were first allowed across the border, but we've only been to the West twice.

Siegfried wants to go to Bavaria on Sunday, the day after tomorrow. They've planned that when Frieda comes home, he'll go back with Hartmut for a week and visit a Demeter farm. He's completely obsessed by the idea. Johannes will have to cover for his father, and there's also Alfred. It will make him feel important for a change.

My work begins on Monday too. The landlord will show me the ropes and then I'll start properly on Tuesday. I'm glad to be doing this; it'll take my mind off things and

I'll be earning my own money.

Marianne helps me wash up. Today she smells just like Gisela; she must have asked what the name of that perfume was. When we've finished she strokes my hair and says, 'You've become a real help, Maria,' and that makes me feel dreadful all over again.

13

August is my favourite month. The heat is still there, but it's not oppressive like July. I become faintly wistful when summer veers towards autumn and my birthday is around the corner. I'm going to be seventeen, and with each passing year I have a greater sense of my significance in the world. But now that our world has become so much larger, this feeling of importance is once again on the wane. On the farm I know I'm needed at least, although they'd get by fine without me.

I've hatched a clever plan: I'm going to spend my birthday with Henner. The timing works rather well. I'll have breakfast with the Brendels, and then Johannes will have to work all day because Siegfried will be away. After that I'll go and see my mother for an hour or two. I'll tell her that if I don't get back to the farm, Johannes will be sad. She'll understand. Then I'll make my way across the fields, through the corn, which is now at waist height, and down the valley to his farm.

★　★　★

Frieda arrives home today. We're all dying to hear what she has to say. But when she finally gets here she looks quite unwell and goes to lie down in her room. Hartmut says she's been tetchy for a few days, she hasn't even wanted to eat properly. I imagine a trip to Bavaria must be pretty major for someone like Frieda, who has spent her whole life on the farm, never going further than the county town apart from one trip to the Baltic. And it turns out I'm right. Later she tells us how uncomfortable she felt so far from home, in Hartmut's guest room amongst all that modern furniture. She was anxious, and she missed Alfred. Alfred, of all people! She's overjoyed to be home, and by the evening she's back to her old self. 'Did you do all the cooking, Maria?' she asks. This is the first time she hasn't addressed me in the third person.

It's Monday. Siegfried has gone and I'm on my way to the tavern, which is not open today apart from to the regulars. My first customers are the village drunks, and I'm delighted to see that Henner is not among them.

There's very little to do, just the same round over and over again: a schnapps, a beer and the occasional plate of raw mince with egg and onions.

After two hours the landlord reckons I've

mastered the basics, so he sends me home. The day is still young, Johannes is grafting in the animal sheds, and I read the story of the Karamazov brothers almost to the end.

Now I understand why Henner was pleased when I said I preferred Grushenka to Katarina Ivanov, despite the fact that she can be quite wicked. Dmitry is sentenced to twenty years in a Siberian camp and Katarina visits him, even though she testified against him in court. All of a sudden Grushenka appears, and Katarina begs her forgiveness. Grushenka replies, 'We're wicked, my dear girl, you and I! We're both wicked! How then are we to forgive one another — you me and I you? Just save him and I'll worship you all my life.' So she intends only to thank Katarina, not forgive her. Dmitry is plunged into despair, but Grushenka says, 'It's her proud lips that spoke and not her heart . . . If she saves you, I'll forgive her everything.'

That's what Henner wants. The heart, not the pride.

But I save the final chapter, the funeral of Little Ilyusha, for later.

★   ★   ★

In the evening Johannes is so exhausted that he can barely stand. Hard labour on the farm is not his thing. I think Siegfried knows this, which is why he's letting him go. He's a reasonable man. Even Johannes' hands are different from his father's. Narrow, pale and soft. Unlike Siegfried, when Johannes wields the pitchfork it doesn't look natural. You could say we have no say in the matter; our bodies are predetermined from the outset. Johannes' hands, Siegfried's paws, my own body, which just now seems to have been made for Henner alone.

I think of his hands, which are like Siegfried's, but also quite different. They're waiting to caress me.

★   ★   ★

Down below, Alfred is sitting idly on the bench. He seems happier, now that his Frieda is home. What binds them is their secret, a secret they will never disclose.

It's peaceful on the farm tonight. There's not a breath of wind in the leaves of the old chestnut tree. The cat is lying at Alfred's feet. Johannes is asleep, Lukas went to bed ages ago, Frieda is recovering from her adventure, and at last Marianne has the chance to leaf through her magazines, which recently she's been hiding from Siegfried. The chickens are still running around, even though it's dark. I think about chasing them into the shed, but then assume Alfred is going to do it, so I get into bed beside Johannes.

When I wander out into the yard the next morning, Marianne is crying on the bench. Her elbows are propped on her legs and her face is buried in her hands. She's sobbing so loudly that it's not long before Alfred and Frieda appear at the windows. Then I see the catastrophe with my own eyes: a fox has been and all the chickens are dead.

Worst of all is that it should happen now, while Siegfried is away and Marianne is in charge. He has his views on women, one of which is that you can't trust them to do things by themselves, or everything goes belly-up. That's unfair, but he won't be argued with. We wonder what we should do, and Johannes suggests that we buy new chickens. But this sets off Marianne again, and she says, 'He'd notice at once. Come on, he knows every animal here personally.' She really does say 'personally', and for some reason this makes me want to laugh, but I hold myself together as best I can.

Eventually I head over to the tavern to start my shift, and from there I call Hartmut. I can scarcely believe that we'll soon have our own telephone line. It seems like the height of luxury, and I make a promise to myself never to forget this time, when it was different. Hartmut isn't at home, but Siegfried comes to the phone and listens in silence as I tell him what happened. I didn't think he would say much, and I was right. 'You just can't trust them to do things by themselves,' he says after a lengthy pause. Then he hangs up. The entire day is under a cloud.

When I get back to the farm that evening I see a car in the drive I don't recognise. It's my father; he's sitting on the bench waiting for me.

I should say about my father that he isn't really a father at all.

I remember very little. I was always told that Dad was away working, and when he came home on leave the arguments would start again almost immediately. Perhaps Mum started them too; at any rate there was a lot of shouting. What I most remember about him is that he was never there. He seldom lived with us although they were married. First came the work trips, then the Russian gas pipeline. On leave he was permanently restless, pacing up and down, going for long walks in the woods. Even on the coldest winter days, he insisted the barbecue was lit in the garden. It was a habit he picked up in Russia, where they barbecued all the time. Vodka kept the men warm and the women wore thick fur coats. Oh yes, the women. When he was home on leave he'd often go into town to buy ladies' underwear. They didn't have enough of it in Russia, he said, and you could sell it easily there. I don't believe he ever sold any.

He didn't even know which year I was in at school, and once, when he made a very poor attempt to try and teach me something, I said, 'I'm not listening to you,' and he replied, 'You're as stupid as your mother.' I can still hear those words today; they've left a painful echo in my mind. Mum kept finding photographs and letters in his pockets. As the pipeline progressed, so the women changed.

I hated him for a long time. His beard, his expression, his small, restless eyes, his hurried way of walking and talking — I hated everything about him. I only ever saw my mother looking depressed. She went around in a haze of sadness, which then stole over me too and gnawed away at my soul with increasing ferocity. I knew I'd never be rid of it.

Then he built us the house — it was the only time he was with us for a while — but in fact he didn't build it for us as a family, only for my mother and me. It didn't make me any happier because we were alone in it. But when he left for good I felt better. My mother didn't, and I've never understood that.

Later I realised what had driven him away each time: a longing to see the world and its far horizons. The G.D.R. was far too small for that. This little country surrounded by a wall was like an animal in a cage. In Russia, by contrast, everything was expansive, on a vast scale and seemingly endless. There he could breathe more easily than in our village. And the women sweetened the loneliness he suffered, but which he sought time and again.

I forgave him long ago, even though he denied me something which no presents or excuses can make up for: my childhood — this slice of our lives which everyone says is pure bliss. I don't know what such happiness feels like, but the longing for it has not gone away.

Grandma Traudel has often told me that I'm like him; she said I've inherited his restlessness and obstinacy. And there he is, sitting on the bench: Ulrich, my father.

He smiles, jumps up and gives me a hug. Then we go for a little walk.

'Why aren't you living at home any more?' he asks, and his eyes roam across the fields.

'Because I prefer it here,' I say bluntly, and that's enough for him.

'What about you?' I ask. 'I've heard you're getting married again.'

'Yes,' he says, nodding contentedly. 'I'm

going to give it another go. She's a fine girl, Nastja.'

'Just turned nineteen, I heard,' I say, annoyed at the spikiness in my voice, but he doesn't notice.

'Yes. Nineteen. But a fine girl,' he repeats, as if it were an achievement to be a fine girl at nineteen.

'I'm not going to school any more, Dad,' I say, and he looks over at the sawmill, which isn't working today.

'Have you finished then?'

'No, I'm just not going any more.'

He doesn't seem surprised, and says, 'You can still go places even if you don't finish school. Besides, you're eighteen tomorrow; you're old enough to know what you're doing. By the way, I brought you a present.'

'Seventeen,' I say. 'I'm only going to be seventeen.'

'Seventeen?' he sounds astonished. 'Really . . . ? Well, I'm sure you'll do the right thing, Maria.'

'Yes, I'll do the right thing.' In the distance the bullocks are standing by the river, drinking their fill.

I think of Siegfried and how sometimes, with one considered sentence, he announces a decision which no-one is then able to dispute. I feel terribly weak by comparison.

'What about Johannes?' he asks, obviously

trying to change the subject. 'Is that all going well? He's a fine chap, your boyfriend.'

'Yes, he is,' I say flatly. I wonder what Dad would make of Henner. Maybe they'd get on and go drinking together.

'Come on, let's go back. I'll give you your present. Then I'd better be off.'

'Back to Nastja?' I ask, and he nods. Then we cross the fields in silence, past the cows and the new calf, through the barn to his car, a Lada, and he takes out a large present, wrapped in gold paper.

'What have you got planned for tomorrow? Are you going to celebrate with Johannes?' he asks as he opens the car door.

I feel a sudden urge to tell him everything, absolutely everything. He wouldn't reproach me, I know. He's my father. He'd understand. But he's already in the car, speeding away.

14

When I wake up my heart is already pounding. I am seventeen. Johannes got up especially to make me breakfast. We stay in bed and eat fresh rolls with jam, and yoghurt with honey; we drink coffee and orange juice. It's still early, but Johannes has to start work. I hear Marianne grumbling outside — where is he? She can't be expected to do all this on her own! She knows we can hear her. His present to me is a photograph in a frame he made himself. The photo is of me standing by the fence at the back of the vegetable garden. I'm wearing a short dress with a white cardigan, looking towards the railway line. There's a soft, somewhat gloomy light; dusk is approaching. Everything in the picture is blurry, except for my face. I don't know when he took this photo, or rather I don't remember. I thank him profusely and shoo him out into the yard.

Then I fetch my father's present. Another picture. A horribly gaudy, abstract oil painting by some Russian artist. At first all I can see are colours, but gradually shapes emerge from the jumble, arranged around a female form in the centre: a single eye, a heart, a cross. The woman has shining red hair, and she's wearing a summer hat decorated with flowers; its rim merges with a sea of green tones. Her breasts are naked, and to her left I can make out the face of an Orthodox priest. A man is kneeling before the priest, but looking at the woman. There's a large hand around his throat. Then everything blurs into a garish red. I only need to blink and it's a formless mass of colour once more. I feel miserable again, wrap the picture back in its shiny paper and slide it under the bed.

★ ★ ★

I have plenty of time. If I went straight to Henner's we'd have almost twelve hours until dark. But first I have to visit my mother.

Johannes will be busy until dusk at least; he finds the work harder going than his father. I put on my prettiest dress, a bright-green, flared cotton number, tight around the bust and printed with small pink flowers. It's handmade to my design. Grandma Traudel was annoyed that I always wore trousers, probably because she had never worn trousers in her life, not even in the iciest of winters. There are two seamstresses in the village so she bought the material, and I was allowed to choose the style I wanted.

I brush my hair until it shines, then I tie it into a simple bun. On the stairs I bump into Frieda and Alfred, on their way out into the yard. They wish me a happy birthday and Frieda fetches an envelope from the kitchen. It contains twenty western marks.

Then I hurry as fast as I can to my mother's. She's been waiting for me, and there's a bunch of flowers on the table. Traudel and Lorenz are there too. It's almost eight o'clock; as I count the vanishing hours I'm like a cat on a hot tin roof. Mum gives me a book, some spotty tights and a lovely scarf. So I don't keep having to borrow one from Marianne, she tells me. We have cake and chat about nothing in particular. For my sake they're probably trying to avoid the more sensitive subjects. My grandparents also give me an envelope, with exactly the same amount in it as Frieda's.

I shovel in my cake and say over and over again how good it is. And then the lies come to my lips as easily as pleasantries. I no longer recognise myself. I don't even have a bad conscience; my need for Henner is simply too great. Shortly before half past nine I leave the house by the garden door and set off. Past the church and cemetery, past the last few houses in the village and into the woods. The most direct route to the farms goes through the woods, down the cliffs to the river, across the railway bridge and along the tracks to Henner's. Carrying a leather satchel with my presents, I begin my descent. People often come climbing here from town, with ropes and all sorts of equipment, but I don't need any of that. I manoeuvre myself down with the help of small trees that jut out from the rock face. When it gets steep I take off my shoes and do what I did when I was a child. We often clambered up and down here, and only once did someone fall. His name was Heiko, and he broke his collarbone, an arm and both ankles. He was pretty lucky. I get to the bottom unscathed and walk along the railway sleepers to the bridge. I put my right ear to the tracks and can hear the humming of a train in the distance. When it passes I dash over the bridge and across the pasture to the farm. It's taken me less than twenty-five minutes.

But when I reach the gate I realise that Henner doesn't know it's my birthday, or that I'm coming. I wait for a while. My breathing returns to normal and I listen for a sign of life from the farm, from this place that spits me out each time, like an unwelcome foreign body.

I can hear the dogs barking. They can't have been far, as the noise is now coming from just the other side of the gate. He'll be here soon, I just need to wait. But it's ages before I hear the crunch of the gravel under his heavy shoes. He opens the gate a little way and pulls me in before closing it again. Each time I enter his realm, I don't know who I will be when I leave it. Outside the world is renewing itself, but here time stands still.

Henner pushes me into the house and up the stairs to a room I've never seen before. It's his mother's bedroom. The bed is by the window and the walls are lined with bookshelves from floor to ceiling. Unusually for them, the villagers haven't exaggerated on this score.

In the right-hand corner is a tiled stove, and there's a stripy woven carpet on the floor. The bed has been freshly made. He sits me on its edge and positions himself between my legs. He looks down at me, one hand lifting my head, the other undoing his trousers. Just this movement, the certainty of his desire, makes me feel light-headed and erases everything from my mind. I am pure emotion.

★ ★ ★

It's only later that we find words again, only once our bodies have spoken. I tell him I am seventeen now, a woman, but he just smiles. It's not yet midday. We lie there quietly, his right arm around me, our feet stroking each other. I'm worried that he may have spoiled me for ever; what can possibly follow a feeling like this? I've never been so happy. My body twitches and shudders, and I snuggle up to him more closely. I feel as if he has pre-empted something.

Henner jolts me out of my thoughts; he suggests we take a trip somewhere.

The old Volga stands by the gate. A miracle it still goes; the car is older than I am. He only bought it recently. I don't ask where we're going, I don't care in the slightest. We drive along the narrow track until we reach the road, and then turn left. That way we don't have to pass the Brendels' farm or the tavern. I'm tired, and the constant humming and rocking of the car eventually lulls me to sleep. When I wake up we're almost at the border. To the right and left are the watchtowers with their sniper posts, but they're no longer occupied. I can see the checkpoint in front of us. We stop briefly, show our I.D. cards, the border guard nods, his gaze wanders from me to Henner and back again, then we drive straight through. I still find it hard to believe, this freedom of movement. What is happening here and what it means for all of us is only slowly dawning on me. Henner is more important than anything now, all my thoughts and feelings are reserved for him.

We drive for a good hour until we come to a small town. We park the car in a side street, then get out and walk. Henner is wearing his dusty shoes and stained trousers. For once his shirt is a gleaming white. He has his hands in his pockets and he says nothing. We stroll through a wide pedestrian zone with a huge number of shops on either side. People are sitting out in cafés, and some of them stare at us. I can sense their eyes in my back. They must think he's my father, and I urgently feel the need to touch him. But I don't.

Henner asks me whether I'd like to buy something; he wants to give me a present, a dress perhaps. I look at women and girls we pass and wonder what I would have to buy to look a little more like them. He walks beside me, his gaze fixed inwards; he doesn't notice them, the other women. For the moment we are enough for each other. I don't need a new dress.

★　★　★

He stops further on at a café in a small square with a fountain. We sit at a table. Once again

I find the choice overwhelming, cappuccino, single and double espresso, and normal coffee in a cup or pot. Henner seems just as bewildered, and when the waiter comes I remember the trip to Munich and say, 'Two cappuccinos, please.' We drink slowly and don't say much. His hand is on my leg under the table. Then I have an idea. Just as Johannes did that time, I say I have to go and 'get something'. He doesn't seem bothered, he just says, 'Don't go too far. You don't know your way around here.' But in fact I am gone for some time, because what I'm looking for isn't that easy to find in the West either. Somehow I find that comforting.

When I come back he's standing by the café. His arms are crossed and he's looking out for me. His face is stony. As I approach him he uncrosses his arms and lets them drop lifelessly, but they tense up again and he clenches his fists.

'For Christ's sake, Maria, where were you? I thought something had happened.'

I want to answer him, but without giving away my secret, so I lie: 'I got lost.'

'For Christ's sake, Maria!' But he says nothing more. Then he grabs my hand and pulls me through the crowds, past the colourful displays in shop windows, and now there is something I fancy after all: a pair of shoes I saw when I was on my own. Black with low heels and criss-cross straps. But he's not going to stop, he doesn't say anything either, and we drive home.

On the way back he's grumpy and tight-lipped. I feel awful. From time to time he glances at me, but remains silent. The Volga groans and moans, and he's driving so fast that I'm thrown all over the place when we turn corners. I'm terrified that he might send me straight home.

But at some point after we've crossed the border, on one of our bumpy country roads, he puts his hand on my neck and strokes me with his rough fingertips that feel like cats' tongues. I sigh. We arrive just before five o'clock; we still have three hours.

He relaxes the moment we get back to the farm; the dogs spring up at him and when he closes the gate he shuts out all those things that unsettle him. Then he goes to see the horses in the stables.

I unpack my bag and start cooking. When Gisela was staying with us she gave Marianne a recipe for chicken soup which she said is delicious. It's meant to be for women who have just given birth, she said, but that doesn't matter — men like it too.

I take two chicken legs, wash them carefully, then put them in a pot with about three litres of water. I add the usual vegetables for soup — carrots, celery, kohlrabi — a few raisins, an apple, three small onions, six cloves of garlic, one leek, and the ingredients I spent an age hunting for, making Henner so worried: lotus root, dates and angelica root. Finally I stir in a heaped dessertspoon of stock powder and some salt, and leave it to cook for two hours. At the end you strain the liquid, discarding everything but the meat, which you take off the bone and chop into small pieces. What you are left with is a clear soup and the meat.

When he enters he stops by the door and sniffs. Then his gaze falls on the apron I found in the cupboard beside the pots and pans, and threw on over my dress. It belonged to his grandmother, who died only a few years ago aged almost ninety. He comes over, twirls me around, laughs and says, 'I like that.' And while the soup is cooking we go back up to the room with the books.

★　★　★

Later I dress slowly. The apron is on the floor by the bed and I leave it there. He's standing by the window, looking at me. There's a hint of sadness in his face, but this may just be the dimness of the evening light.

141

We go downstairs to the kitchen and I serve the soup. He's sitting at the table, reading a book. I say, 'Read it to me, Henner!'

His voice is soft, he articulates the words slowly and deliberately: 'These lonely people, so raw and so driven by their urges, but full of goodness to one another, to the animals and to the earth.'

'I really like that,' I interrupt him, wanting to know the name of the book, but he says, 'Come again soon. Then I'll tell you.' With a smile he sets the book aside.

Henner finds this mothers' soup 'exquisite', as he emphatically puts it. He adds that he's never tasted a chicken soup like it. I act as if this were perfectly normal; I don't want to show how delighted I am. But when I leave his house later on, I'm bursting with pride.

15

My pride evaporates on the way back to the Brendels'; I feel sordid and cruel. Johannes is waiting for his girlfriend, Frieda has probably prepared dinner, but Maria is sated in every respect. I don't understand how I can deceive these people who have taken me in so warmly, the Brendels. I'm utterly ashamed of myself, but I cannot regret what I have done.

Luckily Johannes is still working in one of the pastures when I get home. But it will be dark in half an hour at most, hardly long enough to wipe the rapture from my face. I saw it myself in the mirror, and Henner said, 'You look completely different, Maria. Much more beautiful.' I wonder whether here on the farm they'll notice it too. But they don't, and in some way that eases my conscience. And yet their cluelessness almost maddens me. Only Alfred's noticed it. At dinner he gives me looks, sending shivers down my spine. I don't believe he's *thought* it. He's *felt* it. He doesn't think much, but he has a good instinct.

My poor Johannes is so tired, and doesn't realise how happy that makes me. His exhaustion is my temporary salvation. Over dinner he tells me that he plans to start on the photographs of the village as soon as Siegfried returns. He's already asked around and most seem quite happy about it. Marianne always goes quiet when she hears him talk about art college. Someone's told her there are drugs in the city.

Johannes brushes this off, saying he's not interested in drugs, and then he turns to his mother and says, 'Does Henner ever come to the shop? I'd like to see if I could go and photograph his farm. I might get some good pictures, what with the dogs, the horses and the old house.' Marianne nods and says she'll ask him the next time he comes. I can't stomach another mouthful. But Johannes is full of ideas, and his tiredness seems to have dissipated. 'Maria,' he says, 'you could come with me. I'm sure Henner wouldn't object to me taking photos of you there.' On the contrary, I think, he'd most certainly object. Alfred is quivering. His ugly face hangs briefly over his bowl of soup, and then his sideways glance cuts me in two. He's going to come out with it, I think. It's all over. Part of me would be delighted to be rid of this unbearable tension. He slurps up his soup slowly, and I look him brazenly in the eye until he lowers his head again. Now Johannes is really fired up. 'Maria,' he says, 'they'd be fantastic photos in that old house. Everything looks like it did in the old days, he hasn't even got a bathroom, only an old washbasin, and it's his grandparents' furniture, isn't it, Mum?'

'Yes, you're right,' she says, and I can see the ideas buzzing round his head. Frieda says that Henner still fetches his water from the well in the yard. No wonder his wife didn't fancy hanging around. The flowers trembling in the chill of death, waiting to be mown down, I think, but I must have said it out loud, because Johannes asks, 'What did you say?' Marianne looks at me inquisitively, and so I have to repeat it. I give them the whole verse: 'We are the wanderers without goal, / The clouds blown away by the wind, / The flowers trembling in the chill of death, / Waiting to be mown down.' Marianne says it's a bit morbid, but Johannes finds it beautiful. He asks me how I know it. Keeping my eyes on Alfred I say, 'I read it at my mother's; I spent the day there.' But Alfred goes on eating and doesn't look at me again. The cat slithers around my legs, and its purring sounds like rumbling thunder. Outside the birds are singing.

I'm a terrible liar, I think, and a truly terrible person. I hear the others as if they're far in the distance. I can feel the cat's tongue on my leg, which awakens a memory. Alfred laughs suddenly and Frieda joins in. I don't have a clue what they're laughing about, but in my ears it is a diabolical sound. The only reason he's saying nothing is to torture me, I now think; he wants to savour it to the very end, until everything has to come out. He is a monster. All at once I am revolted by his fawning love for Frieda. But I can also understand why he's so bitter and twisted — a man who always got the short end of the stick, who once upon a time might have been given the opportunity to run the farm himself. He can't take it out on any of the others; this is his home, after all, and Frieda would never forgive him if he did anything to harm Siegfried or Marianne. But I don't belong here. No-one would blame him for it; I imagine they'd even be thankful if he opened their eyes to the real Maria.

Now the cat jumps onto my lap and rubs up against me. You never know where you stand with cats. Johannes says, 'Come on, let's go upstairs.' I get up, keeping the cat on my arm, and hope that Johannes will go to sleep quickly.

★　★　★

I've not had the opportunity to go to Henner's for a while. I'm working at the tavern, and Siegfried came back earlier than planned. The chicken massacre made him anxious. And he'd already seen what he wanted to see: a Demeter farm. He gives a brief report, telling us how they offered to put him up for the night — in the dwarf's chamber. The *dwarf's* chamber! And how they still use a plough pulled by an ox. Jesus! You can take it too far. Otherwise, he says, it was pretty impressive, but it wasn't magic, and he could do without all that superstructure stuff — anthroposophy, for God's sake! Basically most things were like they are here, he said: proper feed produced on the farm, no chemicals or drugs, clean, airy animal sheds, cattle out in the fields. Marianne says she could have told him all this anytime, but Siegfried counters by telling her she should spend more time watching the chickens rather than coming out with all these grand statements. She's offended and so shuts up.

Then he tells us how Gisela answers back to Hartmut, and that he would never put up with a wife like that. He's happy to be back. In any case he couldn't relax because he knew that Johannes would only manage to get through half of what needed to be done.

He's been home for barely an hour and he's already back at work. Johannes is released from his chores for the time being, and he takes his first photos of the village. I hope he goes to Henner's last. Maybe it will be all over by then.

Summer is coming to an end, autumn is just around the corner, and I have no idea where my life is heading. The landlord has said I can keep on working at the tavern, but that's not a solution. As soon as he closes the beer garden, it'll only be the real drinkers who come regularly. People from town will only drop in at weekends and every so often there'll be a visit from the local heritage association. There'll be very little to do. Siegfried said I ought to go back to school. At least repeat the year, even if I don't take my final exams. I could stay on at the farm, he said, and his straightforwardness made me happy. It's all too much. I'm groping blindly; either I can't see a single path to take, or there are far too many.

* * *

I want to see him again. He's stopped coming to the shop, which Marianne is surprised at, and I find it strange too. Rumours are going

148

around that there was something he had to sort out in town, but no-one knows exactly what. I'm worried he's going to forget me. Just like that. Today I'll go and see him after work.

16

The landlord counts up my tips. Almost seven marks, plus my wage for eight hours' work, that makes forty-seven. A tidy sum. Johannes and I could go out for the evening. But now, at the road, I take a right turn, walk for another hundred metres and then follow the track to Henner's. By the time I get to the gate my legs are like jelly. I can't see a light on, and the Volga isn't there. All I can hear is the dogs prowling in the yard. I creep around the house, checking to see whether any windows are open, but everything is shut tight. Where could he be at this time? I'm seized by childish jealousy; I turn and go back. I don't want him imagining I've got nothing better to do than think of him. In any case, he's far too old for me. I begin to walk faster, terrified that someone may have seen me, even though nothing's actually happened on this occasion. That would be the ultimate humiliation, being caught out unnecessarily.

Henner! I bet he's with some woman. What else would he be up to this late? As I turn onto the track leading to the Brendels' farm, a car comes across the bridge. I hide behind one of the large limes and wait. It's him, and he's alone.

This makes me so happy that I race home like a madwoman and dash up the stairs to Johannes. I give him a passionate embrace and we make love again.

But the very next morning, before work, I return to Henner's farm and slide a letter under the gate. 'Come tomorrow and buy a few things from Marianne. Say you'll pick them up later because you've got some errands to run. Then I'll bring them to you. Otherwise I don't know how I'll find the excuse to see you. Maria.'

I thought up this plan in the night. Johannes was sleeping like a corpse — he's always so exhausted in the evenings, and he works away at his photography like a man possessed. I can't think of another way. I'll say that after dropping off Henner's things I need to see my mother. My shift doesn't begin until early afternoon; that gives me ages.

★ ★ ★

Ever since I got up I've been listening out for him in the shop. There have been a few customers from the village, but most of them are old women who just want to have a gossip

151

with Marianne. Henner doesn't come. I can't bear it; I gag as I swallow my breakfast, I'm on the verge of tears. He's not coming, he's not coming, he's not coming. And when I get changed and set off for work, he still hasn't been. I run through all the possible scenarios: the dogs ate the letter, the wind swept it away, the horses trampled it into the ground, he's ill, drunk or both. Or — he doesn't want to see me any more. He's simply had enough of me. I find this inconceivable, and yet likely. The thought of it is worse than any fear of being found out.

When I get to the tavern, I throw my bag behind the bar and start my shift. By the end of the day I'm convinced that it's all over between Henner and me. And as well as the emptiness, I feel — but only fleetingly — a flicker of relief.

★ ★ ★

I'm sitting in the garden near the apple tree; my mother is in her deckchair beside me. The mild air is a tonic. As are the peace and quiet, and even my mother. I'm sitting here, peering over the fence, but in fact there's nothing to see.

It's seven days since I wrote that letter. I'm beginning to feel emotions other than pure

152

sorrow. This is the first time I've ever felt lovesick, and there have been moments when I thought it was going to kill me. When people talk about 'a broken heart' I don't think they're exaggerating; it seems perfectly real to me. I've been chain-smoking and I've eaten next to nothing. I wanted to efface myself. Die. Perish. I wanted to vanish. The Brendels have been so good to me, but I've suffered terribly. I've been unable to reveal the true cause of this suffering; I've had to bear it alone. It seems an excessively harsh punishment for what I've done. Every act of kindness has only intensified my pain, every caress from Johannes has brought me to tears. I've blamed it on my parents, my father getting married, Mum being so sad, my wasted year at school. I've been able to find plenty of reasons.

But I still went to work. I would have gone round the bend if I'd stayed on my own up in the spiders' nest. I've heard nothing from him and I haven't seen him. He lives so near, and yet he's become invisible. It occurred to me that he might have died. At least that would have guaranteed me a place in his heart for all eternity. I would rather have seen him dead than think he no longer wanted me.

But in the end all I wanted was to be at home with Mum, and so Johannes drove me there. She was horrified at the sight of me, my deathly pallor and the dark rings around my eyes. I went into the house and up the stairs to my room, and climbed into bed. My mind was overrun with lines from that verse I'm sure I'll never forget: 'flowers . . . chill of death . . . / Waiting to be mown down . . . mown down . . . mown down.' My mother made some tea and Grandma Traudel a bowl of custard, which I always used to ask for when I was ill in bed. I told them it was Dad's visit which was making me feel so miserable, that and the fact that I'd messed up the year at school. It was Henner who taught me how to lie. That was my fourth day without him. Those that followed brought me closer to my mother again. She looked after me just as she used to. A long time ago, when I was a little girl. Now, in my utter desperation, I'm her needy child once more.

Now it's been seven days. Here we are, sitting in the garden. I haven't died, and I'm able to eat again. I can even imagine a future, albeit a dismal one. I close my eyes and feel the sun on my skin. It is tranquil here, thoughts don't dissipate quickly; in the peace of the garden they hang tenaciously in the air. Still I feel dreadfully unhappy.

A car stops on the lane outside. I hear the doorbell followed by a voice I know. He enters the garden by the open back door and walks over to us. 'The Brendels said I should look in on Maria,' he says with great assurance, 'seeing as I was driving past. And Johannes was asking whether she'd like me to bring her back. I expect he's missing her.'

I fetch my things and get into the car.

17

When I've closed the car door, Mum gives
me a wave from the fence. She smiles and
waves, a very slow wave. Then Grandma
Traudel appears, waving and laughing too. I
smile back and raise my hand in goodbye. He
goes round to the other side of the car and
gets in. It is only now that I notice how gaudy
Grandma Traudel's apron is; it looks ridiculous on her. She's still waving, as if we're
never going to see each other again.

He starts the car and we set off. He's
breathing heavily and driving fast. His
coolheadedness in the garden must have
taken real effort. Lying doesn't come as easily
to him as it does to me. He waits until we're
out of the village, then says, 'I'll take you to
the farm. Then I'll go to the Brendels' and
tell them I met your mother, who said you
wanted to be on your own for a few days.
O.K.?' I nod mechanically and realise that I
almost died for no reason.

When we arrive he takes my bag up to his
mother's room. The corners of his mouth are
drooping with tiredness. He says, 'Have a bit
of a lie-down. I'll be back soon, then I'll make

you something to eat.'

But before he goes he gives me a long, tight hug, and I breathe in the sharp odour of lies.

It's the last week of the holidays, the last free days of summer.

I lie on the bed. The apron I wore when I cooked for him is still on the floor. The window is shut and so filthy that you can barely see through it. The bookshelves are covered in dust and the rug is heavily stained. I'm here all alone for the very first time. I've never noticed before how musty it smells, how all these old things are so out of step with the smells of modern life. I can hardly breathe in here. I fetch a bucket and some cloths from the kitchen and start cleaning. I open the windows wide and try to imagine her sitting here, Henner's mother, with a book in her hand. The window looks out onto the yard, which is enclosed on all sides. I'm all alone. The arched brick gateway is like the entrance to a fortress. At Henner's farm it is both protecting and menacing.

The dogs are lying by the feed trough in the shade. Maybe Henner has ordered them to watch over me. I imagine them looking up at the window. I'm happy he came to get me. So happy.

I clean the windows, dust the shelves, mop the floor and shake out the rug. I hang it out of the window and beat it with my hands. Then I hear him coming back. His car hums along the track; he stops, I hear the door closing and his footsteps as he approaches the gate. He's coming home and I'm already here. I call out and wave to him from the window. He holds up his hand against the sun and smiles.

'Come down,' he says. 'I picked up some food at the tavern.'

When we're sitting at the kitchen table he gives me a long, searching look. Then he says, 'What were you thinking, Maria? Just because I was away for three days, you suddenly imagine it's all over? Christ! I just had things to sort out, important things in town. Things to do with money, all kinds of loose ends.' He's still staring at me. I feel embarrassed. My hands are clasped in my lap; I look out of the window.

'When I got back I found your letter,' he continues. 'So the following morning I went over to Marianne's, bought everything I could and then came home and waited for you. But you didn't show up. So I went back to the Brendels' to pick the stuff up myself, and then I found out you were ill and not eating. No-one knew what was wrong with you; they had to get another waitress at the tavern. I went back the next day. Marianne said you weren't there; you'd asked to go to your mother's . . . I waited for days for you to come back. And all of this because, just for once, things didn't go exactly as you had imagined them. Did you really believe I didn't want you any more?' I can see from his eyes and his frown that he's angry.

I say, 'Yes, I did think that. You didn't tell me; I didn't know you'd gone away. I thought you'd had enough of me. I thought I was going to die, Henner, I mean die for real.' I don't want to cry so I stop talking. I just swallow.

We haven't touched our food, and with paternal strictness he orders me to 'Eat up.' After a while he says, 'Dying isn't that easy, my girl. Believe me.'

A noise that sounds like an abortive laugh rises from his gullet. Henner smothers this peculiar sound by clearing his throat. His anger has melted away, and I think he's quite touched. Later he caresses me so tenderly, it feels very different this time. The things he does are to pleasure me alone, and at the end I'm begging him not to stop. Unlike Johannes he wants to know what love sounds like, even if the windows are open.

All night long he holds me tight in his arms, and the next morning I feel happy and whole again.

* * *

I spend four days with him. To begin with I can't help crying. This dramatic shift from wanting to die to feeling so happy is utterly exhausting. We're talking to each other all the time. He tells me he doesn't know where we're going to go from here, but we'll find a way. Somehow. He doesn't go out drinking any more. He talks a lot about his mother. What she looked like — he says she had a fine, sophisticated face, but she hardly ever laughed. He tells how she started drinking more, hiding the bottles at first — in cupboards, under the bed, in the stables and pig sheds — but later she didn't bother. Then she got cancer and just stayed in bed. She refused to go to hospital, and Henner's grandparents could understand why. They were solitary people, outsiders, and his grandfather had said, 'People should die at home. Besides, we can't keep driving to hospital.' Henner was fifteen at the time. He would often sit on her bed and read to her. He read entire books, from start to finish, and he was there when she died. Shortly before, she sent him out of the room and called for his father. After all these years she now wanted to tell him the story about the Russians. Henner stood behind the door and listened.

You could trace everything back to her rape by those Russians; she was never able to get over the experience. It deeply affected Henner. Whenever he talks about her, he goes rigid and gets very angry. And yet he always brings the subject up. We don't sleep in her room any more, but downstairs, next to the kitchen, where he took me for the first time. From there I sometimes look across to the Brendels' farm; I don't know how I'm ever going to be able to go back there.

I tell him I'm sure Alfred knows everything, but this doesn't bother Henner. It will have to come out at some point, he says, and the way we're carrying on at the moment is shoddy. I agree with him; these lies are dreadful, but so is the truth. For now I want everything to stay as it is.

I've tidied up the kitchen and laid out a nice tablecloth. I make a cooked lunch, and in the evening there's bread, butter, salami, cheese and a few tomatoes and onions. He often lends a hand, he won't just sit there and be served. I adore these meals together. I feel as though I'm doing something quite normal with him. Everything else that happens between us is so very different from the life I know.

When he's out working, I read. Later I tell him about what I've read, although he knows most of it already. Still, he listens to me attentively, and he always wants to know what I think about this or that character, or who I like best. One time he says, 'You can be so clever sometimes, and then you turn into this stubborn little girl again.' I feel hurt and it makes me fractious, but then we make love and it's all forgotten. He makes love to me differently now. Not with the same fury as in the beginning. And nothing embarrasses him; I've never known that before. He tells me what to do, and he asks me what I like. He never turns out the light; he wants to see everything. He wants me to see everything too; he doesn't want me to look away in shame at the sight of his erection. He keeps telling me that there's nothing bad about what we're doing. It's because of him that I can finally accept this. He's my first *real* lover.

Nobody ever sat me down and told me about the facts of life. Everything I know of love came in whispers from dark corners, snippets from others who knew more. But still, many pieces of the puzzle were missing.

All it takes is for him to brush past me at lunchtime when he comes over to see what I'm cooking, and I want him again. He soon realised this, and he teases me by standing behind and slowly pushing his hand up my skirt, inch by inch. His rough fingers stroke me gently, I feel them inside me, and then suddenly he pulls them away again. He loves it when I beg him to keep going, and he asks, 'Maria, what exactly is it you want me to do. Tell me, tell me what you want . . . ' I whisper, 'Stroke me . . . ' and so he starts over again.

This is all so natural that it fills us with hope.

★ ★ ★

Late afternoon on the third day we go for a ride. This is risky; you can see a long way over the fields from the Brendels'. But we feel invincible. He gives me docile Jella, while he takes a young stallion he's just broken in. We gallop as far as the woods and I struggle to stay in the saddle. But when we reach the cover of the trees, we slow the horses to a trot. It's a beautiful day: mild, bright and fragrant. We haven't a care in the world. Then Henner gives the stallion a gentle kick in the flank and speeds away. Laughing, he turns to look back and fails to see the tree lying right across the path. The stallion backs away from the obstacle and rears up. Henner falls and I am paralysed with horror; I wasn't even able to warn him. I dismount, tie Jella to a tree and run over to him. He has rolled down a gentle slope to the left, and he lies there groaning. Before I reach him he calls out, 'It's nothing, Maria, nothing's happened.' I try to help him up, but I can't. He tells me gruffly that he can manage himself. His left ankle is swollen. Somehow he gets to his feet, hobbles up the slope, drags himself to his horse and climbs on again. Then we ride home.

When we get there the swelling has reached an alarming size. He has to lean on me for support as we go into the house, and he's in a sombre mood. He is unable to stand all evening, and I look after him as well as I can. I fetch ice cubes from the freezer, wrap them in kitchen cloths and put them on his injured ankle. In the cupboard above the kitchen sink I find a pain-relieving ointment which I rub in. I butter some bread, pour a drop of vodka and sit beside him. But he's sullen and tetchy, and says I should sleep upstairs tonight. I don't understand.

Later, wide awake, I can't get it out of my mind that Henner's mother died here in this bed. I'm terrified, so I go down to him anyway. He must have fetched himself the vodka bottle. It's by the bed, two-thirds empty. I think he's asleep. He's lying on his right side, breathing evenly. I get into bed next to him and fold my body into his. He takes hold of me and doesn't let go.

The following morning there's a knock at the door. We stop breathing. Henner is quicker to stir and he gets up slowly. The swelling has gone down slightly; it's still painful, but he can walk. I hear him open the front door, and then I start to shake. It's Johannes. He's come to take pictures; he says he wants to make the most of the morning light. Henner is calm and tells Johannes he's welcome to take photos around the farmyard, but he doesn't want him coming into the house today. I sneak into the kitchen, and from there up the stairs to his mother's bedroom. From behind the curtain I watch Johannes wandering around with his camera, seeking out the best angles. I want to die on the spot all over again. The thought of being discovered strikes me as so dreadful that I'd rather starve to death right here than go downstairs. I can hear Henner clattering about in the kitchen. Then, after what seems like an eternity, he brings me some coffee and bread. He puts his finger to his lips, as if he were afraid I might make a noise which would give us away. But we sit there, absolutely silent. Johannes goes into the stables, then out again, to the well, and over to the barn. He takes pictures of the house and animal sheds, of the front door and the arched gateway, of the dogs and the bench by the kitchen window. I can't resist; I peep out from behind the curtain and look down at him. That's when it happens: he points the camera slightly upwards and releases the shutter. I throw myself onto the bed.

'What is it?' Henner whispers, and I reply, 'He took a picture of me.'

'What do you mean?' he asks with a gasp, and I say, 'He pointed the camera up and I think I might be in the picture.'

'Christ Almighty, Maria!' he says, 'That was really stupid!'

Then Johannes calls to Henner. I sit on the floor by the open window, trying to make out what's being said. Johannes asks whether he could come back another time, with Maria, and take photos in the house. Maybe Henner would like one of the pictures. And what's up with his foot — is that a limp? Henner is grumpy. He gives curt answers and Johannes leaves. The gate is closed and bolted behind him. Henner shuffles back to the house and sits at the kitchen table. After a while I come downstairs and sit with him.

A dogged silence.

'But it's not my fault Johannes came,' I insist. He looks at me, as if to say something, but the words evaporate on his lips. I kneel in front of him, lay my head on his thigh and tell him how much I love him. He breathes heavily, pulls me onto his lap and buries his head in my chest. We sit like that for a long time, a long time . . .

18

This time, when I left it was horrible. The fury of his first embraces had been reawakened, and when I was at the gate he hauled me back into the house and threw me onto the bed. He didn't even take my clothes off, he just pulled my dress up and my knickers down, tossing them somewhere. His heavy body buried me in the pillows and covers, I could hardly breathe. He really hurt me. I was almost crushed beneath his weight; there was something bestial, irrational about his desire, something which reminded me of things that must have happened long before my time, things I could not know and yet think I do know, as if my memory were only part of a larger collective one. I pushed my head back for air. I pressed my clenched fists to my chest. When I tried to say something he put his hand over my mouth and whispered in a peculiar voice, 'Be quiet!' His trousers were around his knees, he forced my legs apart, his erection wanted to get inside me. But I closed up.

I really didn't want it this time. I pulled his hand away and said, 'No!' That's all. Then I wriggled off the bed, adjusted my clothes and left.

★ ★ ★

When I arrive at the Brendels', Marianne is standing outside the shop chatting to the landlord's wife. Johannes is nowhere to be seen. Alfred comes towards me across the yard carrying a bucket. He greets me warmly and asks, 'So, did you have a good rest at your mother's? You've put on a bit of weight. Well, it's the right thing to do, to let your mother look after you when you've got problems.' His mouth twists into a crooked grin, and then he carries on with his work. Marianne gets me a glass of fresh milk and puts it on the kitchen table. 'Johannes is upstairs in the darkroom,' she says, and the layer of cream swimming on top of the milk almost makes me sick. But I drink it down and go upstairs.

I knock gingerly. 'Wait a moment,' he calls out, 'I'm almost done!' But it's several minutes before he opens the door. Wet prints are hanging from pegs. He puts his arms around me and strokes my face. 'Are you feeling better?' he asks. 'Have you come back to stay?' and I mumble, 'Yes, everything's fine again.' Then he wastes no time in showing me the pictures. The ones from Henner's farm are there too. He shows me one after the other, explaining *how* he took it and why he took it *like that*. I listen patiently, waiting for the moment when he discovers the woman in the window and everything comes out. We finally get to that photo. The picture is not especially good — slightly blurred and dark — but you can definitely make out a female figure behind the curtain. Johannes sees it too and falls silent. I can sense every nerve in my body; I can feel my mouth stiffen and it's getting more difficult to swallow.

Johannes just stares, and I want to tell him everything. I'm going to tell him the whole truth, then I'll get my bag and go back to Henner. That's how I want to do it.

Johannes turns the picture a fraction. Then he smiles and says, 'Look, there's a woman at the window. Now I know why he wouldn't let me in the house. He didn't want me to see her . . . Shame you can't really tell who it is behind the curtain . . . I don't know what women see in him. Do you get it?' 'No,' I say flatly. I don't know how long I'll be able to go on like this, how far you can spin out a lie. But I suspect it will be for longer than I'd ever imagined.

⋆   ⋆   ⋆

Some quiet days follow. I help Frieda in the kitchen and I do a lot of reading. Sometimes I gaze over at Henner's farm, but there's nothing in particular to see. The day after I came back, Siegfried took me aside at lunchtime and said, 'We need to talk about school, Maria. It starts again next week. I've spoken to Marianne. You can stay with us, but on condition that you go to school — you need to get your exams.'

I let him say his piece, and even though I've made my mind up long ago I play at being obstinate. When I start yet another sentence with 'But . . . ', Siegfried interrupts me and says there are no buts. I feel so grateful to him for his advice.

Then I wander around the yard, looking for something to do. It's all a bit of a mess; there are tools leaning against the wall beneath the overhang of the barn roof: manure forks and pitchforks, shovels, rakes, an old scythe, wheelbarrows, a worn-out tractor tyre and plenty more. The yard is full of hay and chicken droppings. I fetch a large broom and sweep everything towards the gate. Frieda watches from the kitchen window, nods her approval and asks me to get some onions later from the vegetable garden for dinner. Siegfried wants fried potatoes with bacon. Marianne is going around with a large watering can, emptying litres of water into her enormous plant pots. She is humming to herself, and occasionally she picks off the dead leaves. Whenever Siegfried appears she acts as if she's terribly busy, but when she's alone she'll sometimes sit on the bench beneath the chestnuts and close her eyes.

I stand still in a cloud of hay and dust, breathing in the air. The work on the farm is good for me. I can see immediate results — unlike with school. My tiredness at the end of the day is intense and physical, and I sleep deeply.

Several days pass like this; I'm taking a break from Henner.

★   ★   ★

On the evening of 31 August, a Friday, we're sitting watching the news on television. They've signed the unification treaty; the G.D.R. is joining the Federal Republic. We will be one country. But Siegfried looks anxious and says, 'They can't just impose their system on us overnight. It needs to be a slow process of transition, or everything here will fall to pieces.' 'Don't start,' Marianne says, gesturing at him dismissively. 'Why can't you just be happy about it?' But he shakes his head and says, 'It can't work like that. Soon there won't be any farms here, if we're all forced to operate like they do over there.'

I'm finding it hard to concentrate. I keep getting distracted, wondering whether Henner's watching TV too, but I've never noticed one at his house. The reunification ceremony is to take place on 3 October. After that date the G.D.R. will cease to exist. How weird. The country we were all born in is just going to disintegrate, vanish, never to return. Johannes is in a state of great excitement and has a little too much to drink. I think he's happy. In fact Siegfried doesn't look too unhappy either, but he always has to have something to grumble about. Marianne changes the subject and says she's desperate to see the Bavarian Alps. Hartmut and Gisela have said they're welcome any time, but they're coming to us again for reunification. Johannes is feverish; he wants to celebrate reunification in a big city, not here in the village. Frieda and Alfred throw in the odd 'Ah' or 'Hmm', and Lukas seems a little bored. But Siegfried doesn't let him go to his room. 'You should always remember this. It's a historic moment.'

Now I'm feeling in a celebratory mood, and we all stop talking for a while to listen to the newsreader. It's always been the same woman. She used to report on sessions in parliament and the fulfilment of five-year plans.

All of a sudden Siegfried leaps out of his chair. He paces once around the room, sits back down and says, 'The machinery Höfer's got in his mill over in F. dates from before the war. If he's forced to comply with Western regulations then he's done for. And it's the same at the paper factory — you know how ancient those machines are, Marianne. Don't forget, I've been over there at Hartmut's and I've seen that biodynamic farm. They've got completely different rules and regulations. Just the safety legislation alone . . . It's not going to work. I swear, soon it's not just going to be the people at the chemical factory without a job.' He's seething and talking at the top of his voice. Marianne's annoyed that he's ruining the moment for her. She turns down the volume on the television a little and says, 'But you were always having a go at the G.D.R. Is there really nothing about it that makes you happy?'

'Of course there is,' he thunders. 'That's not the point . . . but the future is going to be very different.'

'I don't understand what you're saying, Siegfried. Give it a bit of time, will you? Nobody can predict the future.'

Now Siegfried is sitting at the table. In a

calmer voice, he says, 'It's not hard to predict the future for Höfer's mill. He'll have shut down in six months. Guaranteed.'

He shakes his head, adding, 'We can't rush through in a matter of months what they've taken decades to develop over there. That's just nonsense, Marianne.'

Now we're all feeling on edge. Johannes gives me a sign and we leave the room. As we are going upstairs he says that his father is right, but still, it's a good thing.

19

It is the beginning of September and I'm going to school again. In the mornings Johannes takes me to the bus stop on his motorbike, in the afternoons I walk back. I have to repeat the class and so I'm a year older than the others. The things the girls talk about seem so remote to me. Like how they kissed a boy for the first time in the summer holidays, or how a boy tried to touch one girl's breasts. They giggle coyly, finding it all a bit indecent. Most of them are still fifteen. I was probably like that at their age. The boys shun me. In fact they don't talk to me at all.

I'm an outsider. I've done things with Henner they've never even heard of. There is a huge gulf between us. They won't bridge this gulf until later, by which time I probably won't be here any more.

The lessons are easy. I mean, I know most of it already. Often I'll have a book under my folder and read for an entire period. There's nobody I can talk to anyway. I might become a bookseller. At least that's something I'd find really interesting.

We all know what Johannes is going to be.

He's photographing like a demon. I'm no longer his principle subject. He's now started taking pictures of the villagers' faces. He wants to have one of Henner too, but he hasn't asked him yet. I haven't seen Henner for a few days, apart from once, when he was driving behind us as Johannes brought me to the bus.

Now I'm walking from the bus stop to the Brendels' farm. It's about three kilometres. To my left are meadows with the river beyond. A wooded hill rises above the far side of the river. The Indian summer blows gossamer strands of spiders' webs across the countryside, and they get caught in my hair. In the field to my right the corn is ripening; I pick a tender cob and eat it. As I walk I feel a greater sense of freedom than I've ever felt before.

A car approaches from the distance. It's so quiet here that you immediately know when something's coming. It passes slowly and stops a few metres ahead. He pushes open the door. 'Get in!' he says; I don't need to be asked twice. He gives me a look out of the corner of his eye, and I return it with a smile. Then we drive on to the Brendels' farm.

Marianne is out by the fence talking to Frieda, who for the last few days has been using a stick to help her get around. When we arrive, Henner winds down the window and says, 'Hello, everybody! I picked up Maria. She's going to come over to the paddock to ride Jella.'

I have no time to be surprised, as he's already put the car into reverse and we're on our way. 'That's fine!' I hear Marianne say. 'I'll tell Johannes.' We drive the short distance to his farm and disappear into the old house. Each time I find this place stranger, because outside everything is advancing at such a pace; it's just Henner who isn't. He hasn't been caught up in the flux; he's the same as he ever was.

To begin with he's rough again, because he's hungry for me, he says, adding, 'You come so seldom, Maria, it's not good.' We're standing in the kitchen. It's been a few days, and it could have been longer if he hadn't happened to be driving along that road. It's not merely desire, it's hunger; those are the words he uses. Each time he's seized by this hunger and he wants me so much that his hands and mouth do and say coarse things. It doesn't take long for my desire to equal his. And because he knows this he ignores my token resistance, which I only offer because it seems the proper thing to do, but also because it drives him wild.

I would never concede to Johannes what I

give to Henner instinctively. Why, I cannot say for sure. It wouldn't suit Johannes to be like that, nor am I like that when I'm with him. His passion for his photography is greater than his passion for me. And yet he does love me.

With Henner it's the opposite. His desire is absolute. Everything else follows from that. I can always see straightaway just how much he wants me; I can see it in his eyes and in his expression. His roughness is just as natural as Johannes' tenderness. I no longer find it terrifying. Now I know that it's part of him; making love gently is not Henner's way.

Later he gives me a book which belonged to his mother. That collection of poems with the one that's stayed in my mind. I've rarely been so delighted by a present. The book is old and beautifully bound, and it smells of Henner and the farm. I keep stroking the binding. Inside his mother inscribed her maiden name, Helene Mannsfeld. Carefully I cross it out and write my own name underneath. He smiles and says the book has found a good home; I'll understand the poems, I'll know about the wanderers without a goal . . .

Then I have to go; it's late.

★ ★ ★

Shortly before seven o'clock I'm having supper with the Brendels.

Alfred is sitting opposite me; he asks me how it was at Henner's — he didn't see me riding, even though he might have from where he was up in the meadows by the railway embankment. I say that I went riding in the woods, and then he wants to know whether I was on Jella. I spot the trap and say, no, it was Artus — I fetched him from the stables rather than the paddock — and I rode out to the woods through the cornfield behind the house. 'I see,' Alfred replies. 'I see, so now she's able to ride the young stallion; it wasn't that long ago that she was having trouble on the quiet mare.'

With my mouth full I nod at him and say, 'I've been practising.'

'I see,' he mutters. 'I see . . . ' Apart from Frieda, who gives me an enquiring look, no-one has noticed the edge to his voice. I help myself to more of the cold roast and smile at Alfred.

I find it easier to lie in the evenings. In the mornings, when a cool light illuminates everyone's faces, leaving no shadows, I usually feel dreadful. In the clarity of these early hours my behaviour seems to weigh more heavily, my conscience appears keener, my morals sharper. Later in the day my sense of morality disappears. At night it's non-existent.

★ ★ ★

The landlord asks whether I could come and work this weekend. The local heritage association is having a gathering, and he's going to need more staff. He has a pretty little dance hall beyond the bar, and that's where the meeting is being held. The evening is a real challenge. It always starts harmlessly enough — the chair gives a speech about the beauty of the local area and how important it is to preserve our heritage — but this is just an excuse to drink to excess afterwards. At the start they're all sitting in their seats, chatting to their neighbours. But as the evening progresses, chaos sets in. Sooner or later everyone has moved from their seat and, because we mark all drinks on people's beer mats, we have to run around matching the right beer mat to the right person. Some put their beer mats in their bags, others lose them. It's hopeless.

Many of them wear traditional outfits, and I have to put one on too. Marianne thinks it's fetching, as she put it. But Johannes just makes a face.

They play all the old easy-listening

favourites and sing folk songs. I join in with some of them — the ones I like best — and occasionally one of the elderly men comes and spins me across the dance floor. Then the next one is already waiting and I'm passed around like a trophy. That's when it starts getting dangerous. I have to slap wrists because their hands are everywhere. Much to my irritation, their wives ignore this behaviour. I can only hope it will be over by midnight. Most of them are around sixty, they won't be able to keep at it for much longer.

Just before one o'clock the ballroom is indeed empty, but five stragglers are still sitting at the regulars' table. They've had so much schnapps and beer that even the landlord doesn't think they'll be able to make it home. One of them is Riedel, the former village policeman. He's been retired for two years at least, but he still knows everything that's going on. They say that he had his sights on Henner for years and made life difficult for him. When Henner's wife left, it came out that the police and the Stasi had assigned her to monitor Henner — at least this is the latest version of the story. In his youth Henner was politically active and he used to spend time with a musician called Lutz, who wrote political songs and was later sent to prison. At any rate his problems started when his wife moved in. To begin with everything was normal, but then suddenly the police checks at the farm became more frequent. Henner, Lutz and another friend would sometimes meet up there. This friend purported to be a horse breeder, but in fact he was a set painter for the state theatre. After Ursula, Henner's wife, had been there for a while, the policeman would arrive with a colleague on those very evenings when Henner had company. The colleague was almost certainly with the Stasi. The Stasi may have thought of itself as an entirely secret organisation, but in these villages everyone had a pretty good idea of who worked for them and who didn't.

They confronted Henner with a record of the things he must have said, but only a few people could possibly have heard. He soon worked out the connection between Ursula and the police visits, and he challenged her. She denied everything, but the next morning she disappeared with all her stuff. One drunken evening not long after that, Henner punched Riedel in the face. When they came to the farm to arrest him, he put up one hell of a fight and spent a few weeks in prison. In the end the only thing they could pin on him was a charge of obstructing the police.

Henner never again let a woman stay on his farm for long, and after his spell in prison, his drinking got serious.

There he is at the table, the village policeman, waving his arms and holding forth about how great it is that Germany will soon be one country again. At that moment Henner enters the room. He's stone-cold sober, and he's probably come because of me — he knows what the heritage association is like — but when he sees the policeman he goes straight to his table and sits down.

The old men are drinking whatever they can lay their hands on. Schnapps, vodka, brandy, everything at once. And then something happens. I bring another round to the table, and the policeman puts his hand on my bum and says, 'If I were any younger, I'd have this girl here and now.' He laughs like a nutter. I wriggle from his grasp and go back to the bar. Then Henner stands up. He steps behind the policeman's chair, grabs him by the collar and hauls him to the door. 'Stop that!' the landlord shouts. 'I don't want any trouble here. Go home, Henner, go on, go!'

I run after them, while the others stay sitting as if nothing had happened. They're outside, just by the door, and I really believe Henner's going to kill the policeman. He has his hand around his throat, the policeman is choking, and I say firmly, but in a calm voice, 'Leave him. I'll go home with you right now, but leave him, please — leave him, leave him . . . ' I don't know how often I repeat it, but all of a sudden the policeman is lying there on the ground, retching. Henner takes my wrist and drags me away. He's so incensed that I don't recognise him any more. I try to free myself from his grasp, but he doesn't let me go. He kicks the gate open with his foot and pulls me in. He even kicks the dogs when they greet him, and then he pushes me away. My wrist is hurting like mad. He bolts into the house, sending various things flying. The pan containing the leftovers from lunch hits a wall, and he smashes up a chair. I stay by the door, watching him. I'm not afraid. The worst is over after a few minutes, and the kitchen is in a dreadful state. 'That miserable bastard, that wanker, that fucker . . . ' he spits out again and again, but this outburst eventually fades. When he's ready to sit down, I go to the fridge to fetch vodka, which never runs out here, and half fill two glasses. He drinks slowly, without looking at me, and then he empties my glass too. I go behind him and put my hands on his temples, leaning my head on his. He seems paralysed still, as if he didn't know I was there. His head is slumped forward, there's no tension in his shoulders; he's sunk into himself.

I stand there until I can't take it any more. Then I tell him, 'I'll come back tomorrow. I have to go home now, Johannes is waiting. But I'll be back tomorrow.' I stress the words because I don't think he can hear me. Tomorrow it's Sunday. I have no idea how I'm going to be able to get away from the Brendels' on a Sunday, but that doesn't worry me. Henner has never needed me as much as he does now. He nods and I urge him to go to bed. And he does; he gets up and staggers over to the bedroom. When he lies down, I sit on the edge of the bed and place my hand on his head. He takes my hand and holds it tightly for a while. Then I leave.

* * *

The next morning I sleep in, and by the time I come down for breakfast later than usual, they already know what's happened. The drinking session, the argument, my intervention and how I went home with him. Gabi from the tavern was here to get milk and eggs, and she told them everything.

Johannes asks if I've taken leave of my senses, going home in the middle of the night with Henner, that brutal man — everyone knows how abusive he can get. 'Home . . . '

186

he repeats, slapping his forehead. I hardly know what to say; I splutter and stammer, saying I thought I could calm him down. I was afraid something far worse might happen if I left him alone. Johannes interrupts me and says, 'That's just my point. Something far, far worse might have happened — you and Henner, alone at his house, given the state he was in. You're so naive, Maria, it really gets on my nerves.' I try to justify myself, but it's pointless. They all agree with him. I can count myself lucky that he didn't 'violate' me — that's the word Marianne uses, and she says it over and over again. She seems to like the word, or maybe she's jealous and wouldn't mind being 'violated' by Henner herself. I have bad thoughts when they go on at me like this. What was I doing at his place for so long? The landlord said I was at Henner's for ages. At least an hour, he said, he saw me leave. Any longer and he would have called the police. He could have raped me three times in that hour, I say. And the police couldn't have done a thing about it. As far as I'm concerned, the landlord can go to hell, and that's that.

Neither Alfred nor Frieda says anything, but I can see that Alfred is smiling. I'd love to stuff his half-eaten roll down his throat, and then follow it with another. Siegfried is the only one who talks any sense: 'Henner wouldn't do anything like that; he's not the type.' I'm so grateful to him for that.

After breakfast I gather together a few things and say that I'm going to my mother's. Johannes says he wants to drive me. He's not angry any more, but I am, because of how he talked to me in front of his parents. With a shrug and an awkward wave of his hand he lets me go down the steps, shutting the door behind me. Then I go to Henner's.

★　★　★

In the kitchen everything has been tidied up. There is no reminder of last night. Henner is sitting at the table, eating. When I enter he doesn't stir. He doesn't even raise his eyes. I walk past him almost silently, and take my bag into the room next door. Then I get a chair and sit next to him. He watches me out of the corner of his eye and keeps eating, undeterred.

He should be the first one to say something. I know how to be silent too.

How long do we sit there like that? I don't know.

For a very long time.

I find it hard to gauge time in this house. Sometimes hours are like days, and at others they pass like minutes. But when nothing has happened for what seems like ages and Henner has long since finished eating, I put my hand on his cheek. He groans and looks down at the table. 'I would have killed him,' he says, and when I say nothing he adds, 'and myself too.' Those are words that stand between us like walls.

Now I don't know what's right, but I think what he's saying is true. Then he goes on: 'You don't need me, Maria. You're seventeen! My God, what are you doing here?' He stares at me. It's not that I need to think about it, but I hesitate before saying, 'I want you! I'm old enough; Grandma Traudel was only seventeen. You can't just send me away like that.'

His eyes are still fixed on me. I'd been expecting ridicule, but there's nothing . . .

'I'm not sending you away,' he says. 'I just want to say: you can see what it's like here. You've seen what I'm like. I've got nothing to offer you, nothing at all.' As he speaks he waves his right hand dismissively. I am surprised by how much this affects me. I have to swallow several times before I can say, 'I don't care, I just want to be near you. That's all.' He gives a tired smile and pulls me over to him sluggishly. We sit there, slumped, more silently than the silence on the farm, and for a long time, for a very long time.

We spend the rest of the day in bed. We don't talk much, we just touch each other, and he reads me the last chapter of *The Brothers Karamazov*. At one point Alexey says, 'Certainly we shall rise again, certainly we shall see one another, and shall tell one another gladly and joyfully all that has been.' I want him to repeat it straightaway — it sounds so beautiful, so full of hope — and my delight makes Henner happy too.

20

I'm home by the evening. I don't say much,
apart from that I've still got homework to do,
and go straight upstairs. In the next-door attic
room Selma has given birth to five tiny
kittens, sired by some stray from the village.
Another event that Johannes has immortal-
ised on film. I don't know how many photos
he's taken so far, but it must be in the
hundreds. They're scattered on every surface
and are a reminder that time is passing. His
first pictures have already aged. I look completely different now, something he's noticed
too, but only because of the photographs.
When I'm right in front of him he doesn't
seem to see it at all.

I've arranged with Henner that he picks me
up from school on Tuesdays and Thursdays.
I'll tell Johannes that I'm going into town
with some school friends, or to the park for
an ice cream. Saturdays are when I visit my
mother, and I do actually go to see her in the
mornings, but before lunch I take the path
through the woods to Henner's and stay the
night.

September, with her glorious late-summer

191

days, gently fades. Henner and I have got used to the rhythm of our lies and our love. We see each other regularly, and whenever we drive past the track that leads to the Brendels' farm, I hide by lying flat on the back seat.

The initial magic has vanished; our meetings have now taken on the comfort of routine. He no longer pounces on me the moment I come through the door, and sometimes we just talk. The fear of being discovered has given way to a realisation that the truth doesn't always come to light. It makes me wonder what else goes on in secret that I'll never find out about.

I'm not working at the tavern any more. The landlord would have been quite happy to wait and see if Henner was going to rape me. When I tell this to Henner, he becomes sullen and says, 'So that's what the creep thinks of me, is it?' But Henner has never been bothered by what people say about him.

He seems in good spirits; he's sorting things out on the farm, repairing fences, looking after the horses and planning to renovate parts of the house. It's not true that he still fetches his water from the well; he only does this in summer. He's on the mains like everyone else and he even has a boiler.

I help him clean and tidy up the house: I clean windows, wash curtains, scrub floors and wipe years of dust from cupboards and shelves. He's astonished when he sees what I've done and showers me with endless praise until I turn bright red with happiness.

I could live like this, I think.

At his farm we hear nothing of political events. He really doesn't have a television or a radio, only a record player, but we don't put that on either. There's no time for it during the week, and on our Saturdays we read to each other from books. Henner is an artist manqué. When I tell him this he laughs, but it's a bitter laugh. Hardly surprising that he has no friends in the village. They don't like oddballs, particularly not the kind that read a lot of books. They turned a blind eye until he started neglecting the farm. Once upon a time Henner had more animals, as many as you could have on such a small amount of land — cattle, pigs, chickens, and the horses, of course, which stayed. He had to buy in feed; the land he rented out didn't cover the cost of the hay and concentrated feed that was needed.

When Henner's mother died in 1965, his father and grandparents were still on top of things at the farm. His grandfather died eight years later, and his father in 1980. Henner joined the agricultural collective at eighteen and worked in cattle breeding. When he got home in the evenings, he still had things to do on the farm. The collective was not the right place for Henner; headstrong and obstinate, he had endless spats with the others, while all he really wanted to do was run his own farm. And when his grandmother was the only family he had left, this is what he did. He slaved away all on his own but in the end it became too much. One by one he got rid of the animals, until all that was left were the horses. He wouldn't be parted from them; he knew about horses best of all. With the money he received from the sale of the cattle he bought more horses, good studs, and within a few years his stable was known throughout the region. Compared to horses from the West they're supposed to be worthless, but nobody around here believes that.

The Ursula affair happened in 1974, the year after I was born. Henner was in prison while I was being breastfed by my mother. I often think about that.

There is much that separates us and a few things we have in common, which I prefer talking about. Like me, Henner was a Pioneer, but he didn't join the Free German Youth, nor did he take part in the state initiation ceremony. You couldn't call Henner's family enemies of the state — they weren't even political. They just wanted to be left to run their farm in peace. O.K., Henner's mother hated the Russians, but that was for other reasons. I don't think they cared which system they lived under. All they wanted was to be farmers and not have to worry about taking their son to the Pioneer hall every week, to join in with whatever useless stuff went on there.

It was the grandmother who prevented his initiation. As a Catholic, she insisted at the very least that Henner be confirmed in a Protestant church. The nearest Catholic parish was just too far away. He could have had both, of course, the initiation and confirmation, but his grandmother said that one couldn't serve both God and godless idols. She could be a very stubborn woman. The family agreed that the Free German Youth would have been a drain on the boy's time, and understandably so; there were endless events, meetings, parades and holiday camps. The farm couldn't afford to be generous with time off.

I didn't join the Free German Youth either. That was mainly down to David. His fondness for me was conditional: he wasn't interested in anyone who went along with the regime, even though later he fell in love with just such a girl and never said another word to me. By then I didn't care because I'd already met Johannes.

For both Henner and me there was one serious consequence of not joining the organisation: we were barred from taking our school leaving exams and would never be allowed to go to college. For me everything changed when the Wall came down, but for Henner it was all too late.

I don't know whether he would have studied. He was definitely clever enough, but he was torn between the farm and this other, enticing world opened up to him by books. Sometimes he would go into town, and it was there that he first met Lutz and the set painter. With them he could discuss things that nobody at home understood. What might he have done if he'd been seventeen when the Wall came down?

But he doesn't want to pursue the thought. He doesn't like talking about himself. It took ages for me to get this much out of him. He's a funny one, Henner. He knows more about me. The only thing I never tell him is the most important of all.

*　*　*

I now move between the two farms as if it's completely natural. You can become accustomed to anything. The only time I feel a pang of conscience is when Johannes touches my body. I've been saying no recently. He's so easy-going about it, it seems to verge on indifference. This makes me both happy and sad. Could this be true love, because he takes me for what I am?

And Henner? I take him for what he is.

I love Henner. That's what I can't tell him. I really love him, even when he's drunk, even when he says nothing, and especially when he touches me. I love him. It's as simple as that.

21

Changes are afoot at the Brendels' : Siegfried has grand plans.

We're all sitting around the table again and Siegfried is talking more than he has in all the months I've been here. I don't recognise him.

He wants to lease land from the collective and from some people in the village. It needs to be at least thirty hectares, chiefly pasture, a few hectares of arable land and one hectare for growing vegetables. 'I'm planning a thorough crop rotation,' he says solemnly. Nobody knows what this means, so he explains that it's important for the soil and helps keep pests to a minimum. Two years of clover, then wheat, barley, peas, rye, followed by another two years of clover. He also talks about the nitrogen content of the soil and natural fertilisation. But it's not going to be exactly like the Demeter farm. He says he can do without the 'anthroposophic superstructure', which he finds too weird. He intends to increase his cattle holding from a dozen to twenty-five. He wants to process the milk yield into cheese and yoghurt, so they'll install a cheese kitchen in Frieda's rooms upstairs and a storage room in the basement. None of this is magic, as he keeps saying. The animal sheds will have to be converted and he wants a garage for the vehicles. Then the cows need a proper feeding station and the milking stalls will have to be renovated too. He's calculated that he can produce all his own feed on the additional land. Even the concentrated feed the animals need as a supplement to the hay. He wouldn't need silage, as it's apparently not good for unpasteurised cheese.

Marianne gapes in astonishment but says nothing. Frieda and Alfred find it hard to understand what he's saying. Lukas is staring at his father in admiration, while Johannes doesn't know where to look. He must be worried that he won't be able to get away from here after all.

Now Siegfried is thinking aloud. Rather than selling his calves young, he might fatten them up here on the farm, slaughter them after two to three years and sell their meat himself. But it might get tight with the hay. 'What do you think?' he asks.

Silence.

But Siegfried is unstoppable. It's going to mean a huge amount of work for all of us, and when he says 'all' he stares at each of us in the eye. Even me. I don't know what he imagines, and I must have looked pretty stupid, because now he's roaring with laughter and saying, 'Maria's on early milking duty, five a.m., and we're going to get her into cheese-making. As I said, none of it's . . .' — '. . . magic!' Marianne finishes off Siegfried's sentence and slaps him on the shoulder. He laughs and puts a thick slice of salami in his mouth.

I've never seen him like this, Siegfried. He's absolutely euphoric. And the way he's been going on about it, it wouldn't surprise any of us if everything turned out just as he's described.

The chicken population is already bigger than it was before the fox massacre. Siegfried works like an ox, not wasting a second. Even Johannes and Lukas have to get stuck in. These days Marianne hardly ever gossips with the ladies from the village. Thanks to her, the shop now looks gorgeous. Even Alfred has had to change his lackadaisical approach to work, and it keeps him away from the drink.

I've become a fully fledged member of the family. I helped out with the shop renovation — painting the walls, writing signs and making extra space for produce from the farm. Soon Frieda will be baking loaves with our own flour, and her bread is superb. They could add vanilla or other ingredients to the yoghurt; this was my idea. Siegfried's enthusiasm has infected us all.

Now there are flowerpots on either side of the shop entrance and a sign announcing what's on sale today. If all of Siegfried's plans are realised, the shop will be bursting at the seams in a year's time — or two at the most. But he's already thinking about starting a delivery service. In fact, he's thinking far in advance about everything. Johannes and I find it a bit unsettling because we don't know what we're going to be up to in a year's time, or even where we'll be.

Johannes is taking pictures of everything for posterity, and saying that we need to advertise in town.

There is such enthusiasm here at the Brendels', I'm getting carried away with it too.

The approach on the farm is far more businesslike than it was a few months ago. And it's harvest time. Apples, pears, plums and elderberries need to be picked and processed. I opted for the elderberries. The large sprays are heavy with ripe fruits, and I turn them into juice, jelly and jam, which we'll later sell in the shop. Marianne is incredibly grateful to me, as this is painstaking work. But I've found a way of combining the berry harvest with reading so I don't get bored.

I do the same at Henner's. We carry bucketfuls of fruit into the house. For the last few years Gabi from the tavern has taken care of this, as Henner would have let everything rot. I store some of the fruits in the cellar; with the rest I make batches of compote and jam. I asked him to pick up some ingredients in the West: vanilla, cinnamon, ginger and a few others. Everything Gisela told us about. It smells so wonderful in the kitchen that he keeps going out just so that he can come in again. I make us a fruit soup of elderberries, apples, a pinch of cinnamon and lots of sugar. My hands are jet-black from the berries, which makes Johannes wonder. 'It must be at least three days since you cooked up the berries, but your fingers are still black,' he says, and calmly I answer, 'It's like a dye, this elderberry juice.'

★   ★   ★

Things are changing for my mother too. When I go over there one Saturday morning she's sitting at the table eating plums. She looks fresh, not so thin, and her expression is quite different. She runs her hands through her hair and with an unfamiliar ring to her voice says she's got something to tell me. She twiddles a plum in her hand, and eventually says she wants to move, back to where she came from. I don't reply, but I can feel the blood racing to my head and my temples throbbing.

With tears in her eyes she gives me a rather long-winded explanation about how she's finally realised she doesn't belong here, and she never will. Back home — that's how she puts it — back home there's even a job waiting for her. She wrote to her brother, who still lives there, and he wrote back saying that a new hotel is being built, due to open next year. They're going to need a large number of staff, including accountants, and so many people have been leaving the area. She's crying, but still, she looks happy when she tells me. Then she asks whether I'd like to go with her. I can't look her in the eye when I answer her, although I'm absolutely sure what I want to do.

No, I say, I can't go with her. This is where my school is, Johannes, and all the people who mean something to me, apart from her, of course. She starts to weep even more, and I feel so miserable about the scant time we've spent together over the past few months. She doesn't try to change my mind; it would be a waste of time. Then I do my best to convince her that I'll get by fine without her, even though I'll miss her horribly. Besides, it's only five hours by train, and I'll come often, every holiday. But the most important thing is that it's going to be wonderful for her to return finally to the place she's always longed to be.

Yes, she says, it's something she's always wished for, and I can't ever remember having seen her eyes sparkle like this.

It won't be happening quickly, of course. The move is planned for next spring; before then she wants to go and have a look around, visit old friends, write her job application and start preparing everything.

I don't know what to say to her. I'm happy, and yet sad at the same time. I'm worried about not having a refuge any more, no mother to comfort me when I feel miserable. Who's going to do that now? She continues to talk and she talks quickly, saying much more than usual. She keeps brushing the hair from her face and the tears from her eyes. She needs to talk to the Brendels, she says, there are various things to sort out, and I need a bank account for my child benefit and the money she's going to send me every month until I've finished school. So much to think about!

But I'm not thinking about any of it. I'm just wondering who's going to be there when Henner decides he doesn't want me any more. I'm on the verge of telling her everything, but she's still rabbiting on, talking about this new opportunity and her friends, many of whom still live there and — who knows? — there might even be a man among them who'd be right for her. Some of them are divorced now, after all, and back then a fair few of them were after her. 'Ah . . . ' she says, 'it would be wonderful to find someone to love again.'

I can understand exactly what she's saying, and I really hope she does find love. Then I look at the clock; just gone half past twelve. Only a few minutes ago I was regretting that I hadn't spent more time with my mother, but now I'm desperate to leave her, to see a man who would be just the right age for her. I keep telling her she doesn't have to worry about me, and I stress this point. I'll be in good hands at the Brendels', they'll look after me just as well as she would. As I'm saying this I fetch my bag from under the chair, and when she's finally stopped crying I go. In fact I run. The short cut through the woods and down the rocks, across the bridge and along the meadow to the man who's waiting for me.

22

It's now almost one o'clock, an hour later than usual. He's sitting at the table. In front of him is a plate of food, and the table has been laid for a second person. For me. When I come through the door I rush over to him and throw my arms around his neck. And then I cry, as much as my mother did if not more. Far more, it seems. Right now he is everything to me: father, mother, lover, friend, and even my enemy, in a way.

I'm so terrified of losing him, too, that I feel I'm going out of my mind. He has to tell me a hundred times how much he wants me, me and only me. I want to feel it straightaway, put the truth of his claim to the test. I take his hands and push them beneath my dress. He hesitates for a second — but even that is too long for me. Grabbing my bag, I stride back to the door, where he stops me and continues what I had begun. I surrender myself to him with a desperation that surprises us both.

Later, as I lie there exhausted, he looks at me and says, 'You've turned into such a beautiful woman . . . '

It's the first time he's called me a woman. If he knew just how much of a child I feel, he'd probably be disappointed.

Now I have to grow up. Now, at a time when the future holds so much promise, the door of childhood is closing for ever.

So what happens? Nothing. No banging, no crashing, no thunder. Life simply goes on as before, and yet everything is changing. I get up, go downstairs to the kitchen and wash at the old enamel sink; I warm up the lunch we've allowed to get cold and call him. When he comes down the stairs he's smiling, and that makes me happy. It tastes good; Henner can cook too. I try to imagine the winter here: Henner lighting the stove to warm the room, ice crystals forming on the windows, a draught blowing through and me having to put blankets in front of them, the snow sitting heavily on the roof, which is groaning under the burden. Would we get bored? No. Definitely not. I've never needed so little or felt so strongly that I can be satisfied with myself as during the days I spend with him. Eating, sleeping, making love, reading, working. It's nothing more than that, and yet it's everything.

We take life very slowly here at Henner's farm. In the evenings we put candles on the table, open a bottle of wine and smoke. I ask him what he would do if anyone gave away our secret. He says I'd have to come and stay with him for good. In any case, I'm going to have to make a decision sooner or later, certainly by the time I turn eighteen. The wine has gone to my head and now I'm mesmerised by his words, which keep saying to me, 'You're the one I want, you and no-one else.' The possibility of a child crosses my mind for the first time. Henner smiles and begins to speculate about what the child might look like. I think he's keen on the idea. He's never had any children, and it would be so sad to die without leaving a trace of yourself behind.

I've never considered what Henner actually lives off. I mean, he only works at the farm, and horses are expensive.

When I ask him about this he grins and says I ought to let him worry about that. But then he tells me that for the past few years he's been living off the inheritance from his grandparents, who were hardworking and thrifty. He's also given riding lessons, and two of his thoroughbred Trakehner stallions are excellent studs and he can lease them out regularly. On top of that he sells a young horse every year.

Henner has plans for the farm too. He might rent out rooms and start giving riding lessons again.

The house is big, the countryside beautiful,

and I'd be able to look after the guests. Now he's talking himself into a fever, embellishing this fantasy of our future together with all kinds of lovely details. My homemade jam on the table in the breakfast room — everyone's asking who's made it, it's so delicious. And Henner has acquired a few small animals for our guests' children: cats and rabbits. And chickens, definitely chickens. We wouldn't be able to get our eggs from the Brendels'; we'd need our own. We could also open up a little farm shop — I've learned how these things work. Henner goes to fetch another bottle of wine and the dream being concocted in our minds becomes more and more attractive.

Later in bed he strokes my belly, as if the child we spoke about were already there.

That night I dream of my own death. My feet sink into the earth and my body dissolves. There is no pain; it's a pleasant feeling. I'm still breathing, my mind can still think, but that fades too. I wake up and look over at him. He's sleeping, snoring softly. I can't help smiling; snoring like that vanquishes any thoughts of death.

★   ★   ★

The following morning at the Brendels' is pure torture. I mention my mother's plans and ask whether I can stay with them for the time being. Of course you can, they say. Their answer almost cuts me in two. They've no idea who they have sitting amongst them. I become aware of how different my behaviour is when I'm here, how girlish and innocent. Over at Henner's I act the woman. There have been so many times when I've wanted to tell all, and I believe I would have done had their suspicions been aroused. But what would be the result? I'd lose everything. Johannes, his parents, and Henner too, because I'm sure my mother would force me to go with her. No, I can't do it.

Marianne says we all need to help my mother get everything organised properly. Siegfried adds that I'll be able to lend a hand in the afternoons and holidays. Johannes raises his eyebrows. 'Don't get too excited,' he says. 'We don't plan on staying here for ever.'

No, we don't, I think, definitely not for ever.

The conversation turns to the reunification celebrations. We've invited Hartmut and Gisela, this time without the children, who'll be staying in Bavaria with their grandparents. Johannes wants to go to Leipzig, irrespective of whether I join him, and the others are going to the tavern. They're going to charge ten marks entry, which includes a free drink, and lay on a buffet in the dance hall. He's got good business sense, that landlord. The whole village is going to celebrate together. There aren't so many of them, and not everyone will come; the old ones will stay at home in front of the television.

I don't know what I'm going to do. Leipzig sounds fun, and I can't go back to the tavern. Maybe I will find a way to get to Henner's; that's where I'd prefer to be. He has no-one apart from me.

Alfred is giving me that look again, and it makes me shudder. I'd like to know what his intentions are, if he has any. Maybe all he wants is to see me looking worried. I think he likes that. At last he's found someone who's afraid of *him* rather than the other way round. So why should he say anything now? I mean, he must know everything. He could have betrayed us long ago. I peer at him out of the corner of my eye. He's wearing a greasy cap, even though we're sitting at the table *and* it's Sunday. He's missing a number of teeth. His face is furrowed and his skin is like leather. Even on Sundays he wanders about in dirty, dark-blue dungarees. He probably does it to assert his individuality, but nobody seems to mind. Alfred reminds me of a smelly old dog. I'm ashamed to think it, but I just can't stand the man.

I can't stand being here today either. I fidget at the table and half-heartedly poke about in my food. Marianne gives me a stern look, while Siegfried comes straight out with it: 'Don't you like it, Maria?' 'Yes, I do,' I say, even though my stomach is churning.

I'm longing to go to Henner's, but Johannes wants to take me into town; there are some new friends he'd like me to meet. It's the last Sunday in September. The last Sunday before reunification. There's a last time for everything. Often you don't know that it's going to be the last time. But in this case we do.

★ ★ ★

On the way into town I say, 'Three days to go. Then the G.D.R. will cease to exist.'

'It's already ceased to exist,' he answers, and then adds, 'I don't understand why you're saying it in that funny way, as if you were sad about it . . . '

'It's not that,' I explain. 'Sad isn't the right word. Wistful, perhaps. Or melancholic? No, pensive. That's it: pensive.' I look out of the window. The sky has darkened and the odd drop of rain slaps the roof of the Wartburg.

'Now that it's finally over, I keep remembering so many things,' I say. 'All sorts of things — like when we had to throw hand grenades in P.E. rather than balls. But we never questioned it.'

Johannes grins and says, 'So? How far did yours go?'

'Three or four metres at most,' I reply. 'I'd have blown myself up.' We burst out laughing. Johannes has become like a brother. We're close, we keep secrets from our parents, we laugh a lot and we haven't argued for ages. We walk around hand in hand, but when he touches me it never triggers the same sensation that a single glance from Henner can.

We park the Wartburg and walk across the bridge to the castle. A few months ago they opened a pub in the old kitchens; this has become Johannes' hang-out. We spend the entire afternoon and evening there. By the time we get back it's late, and everyone else is already asleep.

We climb the stairs to our rooms and Johannes puts his hand under my dress. In that instant I know I will never sleep with him again. I need to make a decision. What he wants from me belongs to Henner.

23

I don't go to school the next day. In the morning I leave the house as usual, but on the road I turn left and hurry over to Henner's. He's still having breakfast when I arrive. I put my schoolbag on a chair; the dogs growl quietly. He looks startled but pleased, then gets up, comes over to me, takes my hands and gives me a kiss.

'Is everything O.K., Maria?' he says. I nod, crying at the same time, and then I say, 'I'm coming here. For good, I mean. I'm here for good now.' He doesn't react, his expression is blank, his mind fixed inwards. I say it again, 'I can't bear it any longer; I don't want to be there any more. I want to stay here.' He nods almost imperceptibly and I go on talking: 'At some point I'll have to go back and explain everything, fetch my things and also tell my mother. I'll need a day or two . . . It's not easy, Henner, you know that.' He takes a deep breath and frowns. I'd been expecting an outburst of joy, a clear sign to show I'm welcome. But the silence in the room tells me something different. Eventually he says, 'Have you thought this through properly, Maria?

Really properly? Are you absolutely sure?' and I say, 'Yes, yes I have. I have no doubts. None at all!'

He sits down and groans, as if weighed down by an excessive burden. 'Don't think I don't want you, Maria. I want you more than you could imagine.' Now his tone is sombre, he has to force the words from his lips; it looks so painful I can hardly bear it. 'I just don't want you to throw your life away. Are you sure you'd stick it with me . . . ? You don't really know me . . . '

'That's not true, I know you better than you think!' I shout, close to despair.

'Even so, do you imagine anybody in the village would speak to you again? Marianne?' He lets out a sleazy laugh and adds, 'Have you ever been really lonely, Maria? Do you know what that means . . . ? You're seventeen! Other girls of your age go out dancing, they've got friends and parents. You'd have no-one. No-one! Only me.'

'But you said — '

'Yes, I know what I said,' he interrupts. 'And it's all true.'

'Do you love me?' I ask him, not daring to look him in the eye. I know I would spot the lie.

'Yes, I do love you,' he says in a tired voice. 'But that doesn't mean we can live together.'

His icy words slice through me, splitting me apart: one part angry, one part desperate, one part hopeful and one part loving. Then I cry out, 'Why ever not, for Christ's sake?'

'I've already told you!' he shouts back. 'We would be completely isolated! With no-one but each other! You'd have to work hard. No friends. No variety in your life . . . ' After these last words his outstretched hand cuts the air like a falling axe. 'I've lived on my own for so long, Maria. I've got my particular ways and habits. Do you understand? I can't change now. I'm forty! Older than your mother!'

I try to stay calm, I speak more softly when I say, 'I know all that, but we'll find a way. I'm not like other girls of my age. I'm not a child any more, Henner!'

He nods, putting his arms around me. 'I know. I wanted you and I got you. And now you're here . . . but perhaps you should have another serious think about it.'

The gravity in his voice strips me of the certainty I brought with me, but I reply, 'I don't need to; I've been thinking about it for weeks.'

'What if your mother takes you with her?' he asks, abruptly dropping his arms. His embrace had felt so comforting.

'I won't go, simple as that. She can't drag

me with her. I'll just stay here.'

He gets a bottle of vodka from the fridge; I fetch him a glass from the cupboard. 'Do me a favour,' he says firmly. 'Sleep on it. If you still want to come tomorrow, then come. If not . . . ' His lips narrow.

'I will come. I'll definitely come.' I sit on his lap and put my arm around his neck. He takes it away and gives me a rough kiss. I undo his belt and he carries me into the other room. It becomes a battle, as it was in the beginning. I want him to be tender, I want it to feel right; but in his frenzy he tears off my clothes and throws me onto the bed. I lie on my stomach, he twists my arms onto my back and presses his legs between mine. He wheezes into my ear, 'This is what I'm like, Maria, don't you forget that.' Then he flips me onto my back, grips my arms and says it again. I turn away; cold, salty tears run down my glowing cheeks. He says harshly, 'Look at me, Maria . . . Take a good look at me!' Slowly I turn my head towards him, trying to suppress the sobs which convulse my body. He looms over me. His eyes are wide open and full of fear.

I whisper his name repeatedly until he lets me go. He falls on top of me; I'm almost crushed by his heavy body. He lies there limply, puts his arms around me and his hands beneath my head.

I know what he has in mind. He wants me to make the decision. He doesn't want to be the one to say, 'Stay here with me!' He's trying to show me his worst sides, and either I have to love him in spite of these, or I should just go. But I don't go. I gently push him away from me, take one of his hands and hold it to my face. He's still wheezing, and when I make to get up, he suddenly holds me tight again. This time it's different. This time he's afraid I might leave. Again and again I tell him, 'I'm staying here, Henner. I'm staying here in spite of everything.' We lie in bed until the school day is over. I haven't changed my mind. Traudel was seventeen when she married my Grandpa Lorenz, and they're still together. I don't understand why it couldn't work today. Everything is possible, of that I am sure.

Eventually we get up. He gathers my things, strewn about on the floor by the bed, and sits down beside me. 'I was getting along fine here on my own,' he says. 'I was pretty angry with you when you came with me after the accident with your mother. I wasn't expecting it, Maria.' He looks out of the window at the Brendels' farm. 'And I didn't think you'd come back, either . . . It got my hopes up, you know . . . ' He runs his fingers

218

through his hair, his eyes still fixed on the Brendels'.

'But Johannes is better for you,' he says finally.

'No! He's not. I can't go back to him after everything that's happened. I can't sleep with him again after you.'

He turns to me. 'Are you angry about earlier?' I shake my head, even though he did terrify me. Then he stands and says, 'Go. Go and sort out what you need to sort out! I'll come with you if you like.'

'No,' I say. 'I need to do this on my own.'

He brings me to the gate; as I leave he holds my hand especially tight. The dogs trot behind him. He opens the gate just wide enough for me to slip through, puts his shaky hands on my temples and kisses my forehead. 'Come back quickly, Maria!' he whispers urgently. 'I'll be waiting for you!'

As I leave I turn to look back one last time. The gate is closed, the house stands in silence.

★   ★   ★

From now on this house will be my house too. It has endless rooms, a huge cellar, a dusty attic, where secret objects in old cupboards are waiting to be rediscovered. The house has taken me in as a mussel absorbs a grain of sand, integrating me into its ancient organism.

★ ★ ★

I creep unseen into the Brendels' and go straight upstairs. Johannes is in the darkroom. I knock and wait until he lets me in. For several days he's been working non-stop on his portfolio. He's being very secretive about it and no-one knows why. Now I see.

On the wall Johannes has put more photographs of dead children around the ones that were already there. He's been ferreting them out of the attics of elderly people in the village. Above and below them he has arranged pictures of those still living. There was no family in which all of the children died, and some of the older villagers are siblings of one of the children in the photos. This is his project. He's putting them side by side, the dead and the living. Now I understand why he's been so secretive; Frieda would find it morbid, and I'm sure Marianne would have something to say about it too. I don't know what I think. Not any more. I hope the college accepts him. Then he can go away and forget about me.

'Johannes,' I say, 'I need to talk to you.'

He turns and shows me a picture of two old women. Twins. They live in a tiny old house in the village, next door to the co-op. 'Look,' he says. 'Hedwig and Heidrun Ott, from the village. And here . . . ' he holds up another photo. 'Eberhard Ott, died of pneumonia when he was seven. Fell through the ice one winter. Just think: the bed he's lying on here, the one he died in, is still in that house, up in the attic.' He takes another photograph from the pile. 'Here it is. This is superb, Maria. They're bound to take me when they see this.' These days he uses words like superb, or unbelievable, or subtle. Marianne has noticed it too; she says it comes from mixing with those artist friends of his in town. They're the ones who use all that complicated language.

I try again: 'Johannes, I really need to talk to you.'

He can't stop arranging and rearranging photographs and he's about to show me the next one, but I think he must have heard me because he says, 'Let me just finish up here. We'll talk this evening; I'm right in the middle of things now, I've got so many ideas, Maria. I really think they're going to give me a place.'

I go downstairs to the kitchen, where Frieda is baking cakes. Hartmut is coming tomorrow, and there's so much to do. A strange feeling of calm comes over me; I become acutely aware of every detail in this familiar room — the withered flowers on the table, a bowl with fruit, the small flies above it, the sweat beneath Frieda's armpits, flour dust in her hair, a tiny crack in the bowl with the dough, the texture of the tiles on the floor, the humming of the fridge, the smell of animal sheds, yeast and Frieda. I put on an apron and help her with the baking. Soon I'll be doing all this on my own, over at Henner's. I'm going to be his wife, with everything that this entails.

We all sit together again at supper. They're good people, the Brendels, but from tomorrow I won't be living with them any more. Siegfried eats like a horse; he's working so hard. Marianne is looking forward to the celebrations on Wednesday and she's bought a new dress for the occasion; she doesn't want to pale in comparison to Gisela. Johannes isn't really here. He's sitting with us at the table, but his mind is on his photos. Alfred doesn't look at me, he chomps and slurps as usual, but this doesn't bother me now. Everyone around the table is thinking different thoughts. I take a good look at each of them in turn. We'll never be like this again. Tomorrow everything will be different, for me and for them.

I wonder whether they will ever forgive me. I doubt it. For a short while they'll discuss it and vent their outrage. They'll say I'm scandalous, ungrateful, amoral and selfish; then silence will descend, as it always has done. My name will never be mentioned again, just as Hartmut's name wasn't spoken for years, and just as the name of Volker's father will always be Heinrich, even though I'm certain it must be Alfred.

Yes, I'm sure there will be silence. But they won't forgive me.

After supper Johannes disappears back into his darkroom. I wait for him for hours, and when it gets really late I decide that the truth can wait until morning.

★ ★ ★

As dawn is breaking, as I am somewhere between sleep and wakefulness, I hear the sirens. From far away their wailing reaches me in a muddled dream. I get up unsteadily and open the dark-red curtains at the gable window. Images from my dream flash through my mind one final time, then fade and vanish. Before me is the pasture with the sheep, to the left beyond that, the woods, and on the opposite side, Henner's farm. The train line runs between the two.

A train is stationary. On the track by the railway line I can see several vehicles: the police, an ambulance and another car. There are people rushing about, and all of a sudden I catch sight of the dogs. The two of them are sitting in the grass beside the train line. In front of them something has been covered up. It's not particularly large, as far as I can make out. Something dark, a blanket or tarpaulin. I'm not sure.

I get dressed in silence, go quietly, very quietly down the stairs, through the animal sheds and towards the train line. Even as I walk I know what's happened.

The landlord approaches me from a distance. 'Don't go any further, Maria!' he says. 'You don't want to see it . . . ' I walk past without looking at him.

He heard the dogs, they woke him very early this morning. Gabi told him to ignore them and go back to sleep, but he got up and wandered over. The mastiffs were sitting by their master's head, barking. The train dragged his body further down the line. The driver was still sitting in his engine in a dreadful state of shock. The landlord ran back home yelling and called the police. But I can hear how proud he is to have been the one to find Henner. He'll relish telling people about it for years to come. A story like this doesn't come around very often.

No-one knows what happened. Henner

had been drinking, that much is clear. But why he was crossing the tracks just before dawn is a complete mystery. His head ended up on his side of the line. My body is paralysed by numbness. It starts in my head and shoots down to my toes. I keep walking all the same.

I continue to the house. Our house. There is a window open; I climb in. The glass from yesterday is still there, the vodka glass. The bottle beside it is empty. There's an open jar, one of my homemade jams. I stick my finger in and lick it. As if something is guiding me I move through all the rooms we spent time in, made love in. I take two books from his mother's room; I'd have liked to take them all. I pack a few items neatly into a bag sitting beside the wardrobe: one of his unwashed shirts, the empty glass, the cloth next to the kitchen sink, the books and the candlesticks from the table.

I walk to my mother's. I don't feel anything, I just walk.

She's still asleep when I get there. I put the bag beside her bed and lie down next to her. She tells me the rest later. How she saw me when she woke up and asked me what was wrong; how I started crying and could not stop, my body shaking with waves of pain; how I threw myself on the floor, hit my head on the floorboards and started screaming. Then she called the doctor and I was taken to hospital. They told her I'd had a nervous breakdown.

I was transferred to the adolescent psychiatric unit, where I stayed several weeks.

Heavily sedated, I slept right through the reunification celebrations.

★ ★ ★

Sometime later, when I have told my mother and no-one else the truth, I go back to the Brendels'. They only find out the bare minimum: that I had a nervous breakdown but nobody has determined the precise cause. A fragile personality, the mother moving away, an absent father, having to repeat the year at school — all in all, a seventeen-year-old girl experiencing extreme emotions at a turbulent, uncertain time.

This autumn I'll be leaving the Brendels' farm and moving to Leipzig with Johannes. I don't know what I'll do there yet, but I'll find something.

I often think of Alexey, the youngest of the Karamazov brothers, who said that at some point we will all rise and meet again, and tell each other everything.

Absolutely everything.

We do hope that you have enjoyed reading this large print book.

Did you know that all of our titles are available for purchase?

We publish a wide range of high quality large print books including:
Romances, Mysteries, Classics
General Fiction
Non Fiction and Westerns

Special interest titles available in large print are:
The Little Oxford Dictionary
Music Book
Song Book
Hymn Book
Service Book

Also available from us courtesy of Oxford University Press:
Young Readers' Dictionary
(large print edition)
Young Readers' Thesaurus
(large print edition)

For further information or a free brochure, please contact us at:
Ulverscroft Large Print Books Ltd.,
The Green, Bradgate Road, Anstey,
Leicester, LE7 7FU, England.
Tel: (00 44) 0116 236 4325
Fax: (00 44) 0116 234 0205

PROMISE TO OBEY

Stella Whitelaw

When Jessica is charmed by Lucas Coleman into accepting a job at grand Upton Hall, she is not expecting to have to provide full-time care for his autistic son, asthmatic daughter, and the sharp-tongued Lady Grace, who is recuperating from hip replacement surgery — and she certainly did not expect a marriage proposal from her employer. But where is the children's mother? Fighting her attraction to the beguiling Lucas, she is determined to keep her head. A disastrous affair with a London doctor has put her off men; but when he descends on Upton Hall, determined to win her back, Jessica's life is thrown into turmoil.

THE FOREVER OF ELLA AND MICHA

Jessica Sorensen

Ella and Micha have been through tragedy, heartbreak, and love; now they are thousands of miles apart. Ella continues to go to school and tries to deal with her past, desperate for Micha to be by her side, but she refuses to let her problems get in the way of his dreams. Micha spends his days travelling the country with the band. He wants Ella closer to him — but he won't ask her to leave college. The few moments they do spend together are fleeting, intense, and filled with passion. They know they want to be together, but is wanting something enough to get them to their forever?

FRANCES AND BERNARD

Carlene Bauer

He is Bernard Eliot, a poet: passionate, gregarious, a force of nature. She is Frances Reardon, a novelist: wry, uncompromising and quick to skewer. In the summer of 1957, Frances and Bernard meet at a writers' colony. Afterwards, he sends her a letter, and with it begins an almost holy friendship. From their first, witty missives to dispatches from the long, dark night of the soul, Frances and Bernard tussle over faith and family, literature and creativity, madness and devotion — and before long, they are writing the account of their very own love story.